"Are you going to kiss me good-night?"

Holly chuckled. "I wasn't planning on it." They were standing on his porch. The light was on, the Christmas wreath was festive, and the place seemed to be welcoming him home.

"You ask me out, and then you refuse to kiss me good-night?" Tom asked. "If you're worried about rejection, I've already decided it's okay to kiss on the second date."

"Oh, well, in that case..." She put her arms around his waist and leaned her head back. He enfolded her in his arms so that she felt snug and safe and cherished, and then his lips met hers in a kiss of such warmth that she wanted to melt.

"Are you as surprised as I am?" Tom asked huskily.

"It was only going to be a friendly kiss...I really hadn't expected..." The *last* thing Holly expected that Christmas season was to start falling in love.

ABOUT THE AUTHOR

Beverly Sommers's literary career began early. She was only two when her first short story was published in *The New Yorker*. At age six she wrote the critically acclaimed *War and Peace*. After that she sank into relative obscurity until, at the age of eleven, she wrote and directed her first Broadway play, *Hamlet*, the satiric story of a rock star from outer space. When Beverly isn't writing for Harlequin, she spends her time making up tall tales.

Books by Beverly Sommers

HARLEQUIN AMERICAN ROMANCE

152–SNOWBIRD
165–LE CLUB
179–SILENT NIGHT
191–PHOEBE'S DEPUTY
216–OF CATS AND KINGS
242–TEACHER'S PET
258–REACH FOR THE SKY

HARLEQUIN INTRIGUE

3–MISTAKEN IDENTITY
87–HOLD BACK THE NIGHT

Losing
It
Beverly Sommers

Harlequin Books

TORONTO • NEW YORK • LONDON
AMSTERDAM • PARIS • SYDNEY • HAMBURG
STOCKHOLM • ATHENS • TOKYO • MILAN

This is for Phyllis and Sylvia
and the memory of the incredible Gourmet Café,
and for Michael Filan,
leader extraordinaire

Published January 1989

First printing November 1988

ISBN 0-373-16278-2

Prologue

"Let's start with the premise that this is a romance," she said.

"Okay, we could do that."

"You sound less than thrilled."

He chuckled. "Do I?"

"Now you're laughing at me. It is a romance, what else would you call it? We met, we were attracted, we had a few problems—"

"A few?"

"We fell in love..."

"So we did." He started to stuff his pipe, a good sign that he was settling down to a long evening. "But it also had its funny moments."

"And its sad moments, and its poignant moments," she added.

"It's the funny parts I remember best, though."

"All right. We'll call it a romantic comedy, does that suit you?"

"Well enough, I guess. You know more about those things than I do."

"What things?"

"I only meant that you read books. Rather trashy books, if I may say so."

"You may not. At times they have been as necessary to me as breathing."

"Still?"

"Well, maybe not still. But we're getting off the subject." She slid farther down in the couch. "Let's think of a title."

"Must we?" he asked, sending out a stream of pungent-smelling smoke.

"Eventually."

"Something like *Her Jealous Heart's Surrender*? That sort of thing?"

"If you won't be serious—"

"I'm deadly serious. I've caught a look at some of those titles you've sneaked into our cart at the supermarket. If I'm not mistaken, the one currently residing in the bathroom is pretty close to that."

"We'll leave the title for now. Perhaps something will come to us as we go along." She gave a happy little laugh. "This is fun, isn't it?"

"More than a barrel of monkeys."

"Okay, now that's something to watch out for right off. I believe you'd call it a cliché."

"But it was said ironically. I think you can get away with clichés when they're done with an ironic touch."

She started to give him a dubious look, but he looked so pleased with himself that she leaned over and kissed him instead. "All right, what shall we name our main character?"

"We can use my name. I don't mind."

There was a short silence. "The woman is the main character," she pointed out in a diplomatic tone of voice.

"Not from my point of view. I had a distinct feeling while all this was going on that I was the main character."

"That just shows that you don't know what you're talking about, because in these books the woman is always the main character. Sometimes it can be from the man's point of view, but mostly it's from the woman's."

"Is that a tradition that can't be tampered with?"

"I believe so. That's not to say you can't have a lot of input, but I believe I get a little more."

"Well, I guess that's only fair. You do seem to do most of the talking."

She wanted to stay silent then for a very long time so that it would appear that he was the one who did most of the talking, but after about six seconds of silence she couldn't stand it anymore. "I don't want to use my name, and I don't think we should use yours, either. This is supposed to be fiction, you know."

"Yes, but it would hardly matter because no one I know reads those books."

"Well, I know plenty of people who read them, including all of my female relatives. Anyway, I don't want my name. I want a really glamorous name."

"I love your name," he said.

"It's too plain. My mother had run out of all the interesting names when it came to me. How about Diana Trump?"

"As a cross between the princess and the millionaire?"

She laughed. "I thought that sounded familiar as soon as I said it."

"How about something simple yet nice? Maybe Anne."

"Anne? That's boring!"

"I once was in love with this girl named Anne."

She moved away from him on the couch.

"But that was a long time ago."

"You haven't forgotten her, I notice."

"You never forget the ones you truly love."

"Ones? Plural?"

He reached over and put his arm around her shoulders. "I loved her way back in the fifth grade."

"And the others?"

"Well, in the sixth grade there was Tammy, and in the seventh grade I was in love more than once—"

"Forget it," she said, settling back against his arm. "If you're going to start that far back, we'll never get the book started. But not Anne. I want something more interesting."

"Choose what you like, but I'm warning you now. I will not be burdened with one of those ridiculous names like Lance or Damon or Randall. Tom. I'll be called Tom. That's a good, no-nonsense sort of name. I could be a ball player with a name like that."

"You could also be a ball player with a name like Mookie."

He chuckled and pulled her closer. He was crazy about the fact that she knew who Mookie was.

"Tom's fine," she agreed. "I had a crush on a Tom Cunningham in the seventh grade. He was in the eighth grade, though, and didn't even know I existed."

"I like the sound of that," he said, showing no signs of jealousy whatsoever. "Tom Cunningham will suit me fine."

"All right, then I'll be Holly Benson. She was the girl Tom Cunningham was in love with. I envied her

Tom and I envied her name and she was also gorgeous."

"You're gorgeous," he said, saying exactly the right thing.

"Thank you. But I sure wasn't then."

"So, how do we start this off? Do you go first?"

"Yes. It should start with the heroine's point of view. After all, you weren't in it at the very start."

"As far as I'm concerned I was."

"No, I'll have to set it up first. You probably won't even come in until the second chapter."

"Then I can just relax and turn on the ball game?"

"Will my typing bother you?"

"Not at all. Will the ball game bother you?"

She sighed. "Do you really think we can do this? I mean, what do we know about writing?"

"I guess we'll soon find out."

Chapter One

Holly locked the car door and headed for the building at a run. She could remember a time when the cold didn't faze her, when she welcomed winter for its long voluminous coats that hid everything. No more. Now when it was twenty degrees outside it felt like twenty below to her.

She passed the crowded Toys Я Us, the storefront law office with the flashing neon sign, the Chinese take-out place and the tanning parlor that seemed to be doing a record business in the cold weather.

She pushed open the glass door and stood shivering for a moment until the steam heat began to thaw her out. "How are you doing?" she said to Maxine, who was manning the desk. Maxine was dressed in bright red wool with a plastic Santa Claus pinned on her dress and earrings that looked like green Christmas tree ornaments.

"You're late," said Maxine.

"I know, I'm sorry," said Holly in a reflex reaction. She was always late; she was always sorry.

"Been doing your Christmas shopping?" asked Maxine.

Holly shook her head. "No, I'm way behind, as usual. I had to go to jail."

She shrugged off her coat as she passed by the scale and entered the main room. The crowd had their backs to her and were chatting loudly. They sounded as though they were full of holiday cheer or a good meal, and Holly hoped it was the former.

She stood at the back of the room and hung up her coat, her muffler and the extra sweater she wore beneath the coat. She put her gloves in the coat pockets, then leaned down to pull off her leg warmers. They felt good. Even more importantly, she loved the way they looked. But if she kept them on she'd freeze when she went out again.

"There she is. Hi, sweetie," called out Sylvia, her gruff voice rising above the babble and causing a lull in the conversation.

"Hi, how is everybody tonight?" asked Holly, looking over the faces, starting right in before she even reached the podium.

She opened her briefcase, took out her pictures and the notes she had prepared, then turned to the crowd. She gave them the once-over. "I see some new faces tonight. Good for you. Most of us would just wait until after New Year's and make coming here for the first time a New Year's resolution. It takes guts to join a week before Christmas."

"Don't even mention the holidays," said Sylvia. "You think you got a mother who likes to cook? My mother *invented* cooking."

There were a few laughs, then a settling down. Holly put both hands on the sides of the podium, took a deep breath, and wondered what she was doing standing up in front of a bunch of people. Was this the same shy Holly who had been afraid to raise her hand in school when she had to go to the bathroom?

"Good evening, ladies...and Arnold. for those of you who are new to Weight Watchers, my name is Holly and I'm your leader tonight."

"Good evening, Holly," said a few of the old-timers.

"Tonight I'm going to talk about temptation," said Holly. "I'm going to talk about what to do when everyone else is stuffing themselves at the dinner table on Christmas and what to do at holiday parties, particularly New Year's Eve parties."

"Don't go to them," yelled Phyllis.

"But first," said Holly, "my credentials." She held up a picture of herself at her wedding. What she was wearing in the picture wasn't a tent, but it was close to it. "This was me," she said, "before. Before I lost a hundred and forty pounds. I am now at one hundred and six and maintaining."

There was a burst of applause and Holly stepped to the first row and handed her picture to the woman sitting there. "And that picture wasn't even me at my heaviest. I felt almost like a waif that day."

She could hear Sylvia murmuring, "She's a pretty girl, she'll get married again."

Holly stood there a moment in her size four tailored skirt and her size small sweater, beneath which she wore a bra without an underwire, and she suddenly wanted to thank her first leader who had welcomed her so warmly that she kept coming back. She wanted to give the same kind of warmth to these people, even if a few of them, like Sylvia, were there for the socializing more than serious dieting.

"I'm living proof that it works," she told them. "And don't get the idea it was easy for me, because it wasn't. I come from a fat family, I had a husband who wanted me to stay fat, and even today my pulse rate goes up whenever I pass a bakery. But it's possible, it really is."

"Except during the holidays," said Sylvia.

"All right," said Holly. "To start off, does anyone have any news for us?"

Several hands shot up and Holly nodded to Leslie, one of the younger members.

"I lost four and a half pounds," said Leslie, a shy smile on her face. She'd been coming for three months and consistently had a weight loss, and Holly was very proud of her.

There was a lot of applause and Holly joined in.

Several other members gave their weekly weight losses and then Arnold said, "My wife had a baby girl."

"Tell her she'd better be back next week," said Sylvia, which got a lot of laughs.

"Tell her congratulations," said Holly, and there was a round of applause.

"I was good," said Arnold. "I didn't even take her any candy in the hospital." He waited a beat and then said, "We both ate the flowers, though."

Holly waited for the laughter to die down and then said, "Okay, the holidays. I've got a few suggestions for you and then maybe you'll have some you want to share with us. One of the most important things to remember is never go to a party hungry. Eat your meal before you go, and that way you won't be tempted to nibble. Nibbling is disastrous. A little here, a little there, and it all adds up to extra calories. Something

else you can do is cut up some carrot sticks and celery
and take them along with you to parties."

"What about drinks?" asked one of the new members.

"What *about* drinks?" Holly asked the older members.

"Not on week one," said Sylvia.

"I just have Perrier with a twist of lime," said Phyllis.

"A glass of white wine's not going to hurt," said Arnold.

Holly nodded. "If you're going to feel deprived without a drink, then by all means have a glass of white wine. But compensate by not eating something else that day. Another thing, while we're on the subject of holidays. You know all those chocolate Santa Clauses and marshmallow Christmas trees and those peppermint candy canes some of us like to put on our trees? Forget it. Nothing edible should reside on your Christmas tree, and if you're going to buy Christmas candy for the kids' stockings, buy it on Christmas Eve. Don't have it around the house to tempt you."

One of the newcomers raised her hand and asked, "What's Christmas without the goodies?"

"That's a good question," said Holly. "I think a lot of us equate holidays with eating. And I'm not going to give you a lecture about what Christmas really means, because it probably means different things to all of you. Just think of it this way. Instead of thinking of a stocking filled with candy, think of being able to wear panty hose in a smaller size. Not you, Arnold, of course. Instead of thinking of a huge Christmas dinner, think of the pretty Christmas dress you'll be able to wear next year. Don't think, 'I can't have this or that,' think, instead, of what you'll be able to have once you've reached your goal.''

"A whole new wardrobe," said Sylvia.

Several hands shot into the air, and Holly was about to call on Judy when she saw a familiar man walk into the back of the room and stand there. It took her a moment because he was wearing a knitted hat pulled down and a muffler wrapped around the bottom of his face, but then he lowered the muffler and she recognized Bobby. And what in the world was Bobby doing invading one of her meetings?

Because of the lull, one of the members started asking a question without waiting to be called on, but her question faded off as Bobby said, loudly and clearly, "You here to break up a few more marriages, Holly?"

Twenty-one pairs of eyes turned around to see who was speaking from the back of the room. Holly sighed, hoping against hope that Bobby wasn't going to cause a scene.

"Please leave, Bobby," she said firmly, "we're having a meeting here."

Bobby slowly pulled off his cap, releasing a tumble of dark brown curls. He stood holding his hat in front of him, a tentative smile on his face. Bobby was trying to be cute and wasn't succeeding with Holly at all.

"I asked you to leave, Bobby," Holly reiterated, trying to stay calm.

"First you leave me, then you ask me to leave," said Bobby, and Holly could sense the collective indrawn breath.

Bobby turned his smile on the crowd. "I'm her husband," he told them, as though imparting an important message.

Several heads turned to look at Holly before turning back to Bobby.

"He's my *ex*-husband," said Holly. "We're divorced."

"She used to be so sweet," said Bobby. "Then she started going to Weight Watchers and she got meaner and meaner."

"Don't start with me, Bobby," warned Holly. But the warning went unheeded as they always had with him.

"I wish you could've seen her when she married me," said Bobby, and one well-meaning member held up Holly's wedding picture.

Bobby's eyes lit up as he reached out for it, gave it a loving look, then held it high for everyone to see. "That's my Holly when she married me. Wasn't she pretty?"

"Of course she was pretty," said Sylvia, "but now she's stunning."

Bobby hung his head a little. "The only thing stunning about her was the blow she dealt me by walking out on our happy home."

Holly spoke in a low voice, but it reached the back of the room. "Tell them what you used to call me, Bobby. Tell them your pet names for me."

"You mean like 'honey'?" asked Bobby, all innocence.

Holly took a couple of steps around the podium. "I apologize to all of you for the disturbance my ex-husband is creating."

"What'd he call you?" asked Arnold.

"One of his favorite names for me was 'moose,'" she said. Several of the women turned to Bobby with outraged looks. "Another was 'great white whale.' He usually saved that one up to use in front of his friends."

"I didn't mean nothin' by them," said Bobby, sounding properly contrite. "You knew I loved you."

"Not once, not ever," said Holly, "did you make me feel loved. You treated me like a thing, like some possession of yours, and not one of your favorites, either. You treated your electric guitar with a lot more respect."

"I think you'd better leave, young man," said Sylvia.

"I was good enough for you when you were fat, though, wasn't I?" asked Bobby.

"You made me feel like I was worthless," said Holly, "and then, when I began to feel better about myself, began to develop a little self-respect, you started berating me."

Bobby singled out Arnold. "Tell me, what would you think if your wife left your warm bed every morning—half the time when it was still dark out—to go outside and run? I mean, does that make for a good marriage?"

Arnold looked uncomfortable.

"I'm sorry," said Holly, "but I can't allow you to continue this, Bobby. These people have paid good money to come here tonight—"

"We don't mind," said one of the new members, clearly enchanted by the unexpected drama being played out before her eyes.

"I mind," said Holly. "If you don't leave now, Bobby, I'm afraid I'm going to have to call the police and report a disturbance."

"You'd call the police on me?" asked Bobby, his eyes wide in simulated shock.

Holly gave a decisive nod. "Yes."

And then, in a move that turned Holly's knees to jelly and caused several gasps and screams, Bobby reached inside his camel duffle coat and pulled out a handgun. "I don't think anyone's going to call the police," said Bobby.

Several members dove to the floor.

Holly hadn't noticed Maxine looking in the doorway until she let out a scream and then disappeared from sight. A moment later Holly heard the door to the building slam shut.

Holly moved back to the podium and held on to it with both hands. She was in charge, she was responsible for these people, and it was her crazy ex-husband who was holding a gun on them. "Put that away right now, Bobby, before you get into deeper trouble than you're already in."

"I've got a better idea," said Bobby. "We're going to have a little hearing here, sort of like a trial. And when it's all over, you're going to come back to me."

Holly took a deep breath and tried to steady herself. "I think this is private business, Bobby, between you and me. Just let the members leave the building, and then we'll discuss it."

Arnold began to get out of his chair, but Bobby pointed the gun at him and he sat back down. "No one's going anywhere," said Bobby. "You folks are going to hear both sides and then decide who's right."

"I can give you my verdict right now," said Sylvia. "If the only way you can get your wife back is by waving a gun at a room of innocent bystanders—"

"Shut up!" said Bobby, pointing the gun at her. Sylvia, for maybe the first time in her life, shut up.

"I don't know what you're trying to prove," said Holly.

"You gave me no choice, Holly," said Bobby. "You hang up on me when I call. You won't answer your door when I come by. I'm desperate."

Holly tried to assess how desperate he was. Was he desperate enough to shoot someone? Turn the gun on himself? She didn't think so. She didn't think he had the guts. She'd be pretty surprised if the gun was even loaded, although she wasn't going to challenge him in order to find out. It was pure ego with him, nothing more. That and loving being center stage with a rapt audience.

Holly tried a diversion. "I don't know if any of you have seen my ex-husband before," she said. "Any of you ever go to the Skylark Lounge on weekends?"

There were a couple of nods, a few murmurs.

"Well, with his hair slicked back and different clothes...Bobby's the Elvis impersonator, has a show there most Saturday nights."

A few of the middle-aged women turned interested looks in Bobby's direction.

"I'm not here to perform," said Bobby.

"You know 'Blue Suede Shoes'?" asked Arnold.

Holly couldn't help it, she had to smile. She was in a dangerous situation, Bobby might be holding a loaded gun, but the sense of humor that had gotten her into trouble with Bobby before couldn't be stifled. She knew if Arnold said one more word she'd break up. Not Bobby, though. Bobby had never had a sense of humor.

She heard a few chuckles and realized that if Bobby thought they were laughing at him he might fly off the handle. But then she heard another sound, that of a siren. Maxine must have called the police, thank God, and help was on the way.

In order to mask the sound of the sirens from Bobby, she quickly said, "Bobby has real talent. He was runner-up in an Elvis Presley impersonator contest once..." But then she let her words trail off as she could tell that everyone could hear the sirens.

Bobby went to the door and looked out into the reception area. He turned back to them and said, "Any of you move while I go lock the door, someone's going to get hurt."

Nobody moved and Holly said, "Just stay calm, folks, you're doing fine. The police are here and I'm sure they'll have everything under control shortly."

Except that Bobby still had a gun.

Bobby was just coming back into the room when they all heard the voice through the bullhorn: "Release the hostages and come out with your hands in the air!"

"Hostages?" said Bobby, his face crumpling a little.

"Well, what would *you* call it?" Phyllis asked him. "You're holding a gun on us, aren't you?"

"A hostage situation," said Arnold, sounding rather excited.

"This is crazy," said Bobby, getting agitated. He was pacing the back of the room now, making the same quick turns he used on stage with his electric guitar.

"Well, if we're not hostages," said Holly, "then why don't we all leave?"

"Stay where you are," ordered Bobby, looking around. "Is there only one door to this place, Holly?"

"Just the one you locked," said Holly, beginning to feel a little claustrophobic in a room with no windows and a man with a gun. Bobby probably got the gun from one of his wild friends, in which case it could very well be loaded.

"I have to meet my husband at eight o'clock," said one of the new members, sounding frightened.

"Shut up!" yelled Bobby. "No talking. I've got to think!"

There was the sound of more sirens, and once again a voice through the bullhorn. "We have the building surrounded! Release the hostages and come out with your hands up!"

"It's just like TV," said Arnold. "I bet they've got the SWAT team out there."

"I told you to shut up," said Bobby.

"You walk out there now, they're going to gun you down," said an elderly lady in the back row who seemed to be enjoying herself.

Holly left the relative safety of the podium and began to walk slowly toward the back of the room. "Why don't I just go out there, Bobby, and explain to them that it's all a big mistake."

"You'd love to see me gunned down," said Bobby.

"No, Bobby, I would not."

"We could order in food," said Arnold.

"Arnold," said Holly, "I don't think you're helping matters any."

Arnold looked rebuffed. "They always do that in hostage situations. The cops send in food."

"Pizza," said another member. "We could have them order a pizza."

Holly came to a standstill and glared at the member. "Doreen, I think you're forgetting you're at a

Weight Watchers meeting. You are not allowed pizza in your third week. And this is just what I was talking about, just like holiday parties. You can't allow special events to influence your diet."

"We're all in danger, and you're worried about our diet?" asked Arnold.

"I find that no more surprising than the fact that you're worried about food," Holly told him.

The telephone in the outer office began to ring.

"That'll be the hostage negotiator," said Sylvia.

"They must be crazy if they think I'm going to walk out there and let them get a shot at me through the glass door," said Bobby.

"I'll answer it for you," offered Phyllis.

Bobby looked at Holly. "You answer it. But if you try anything funny and somebody gets hurt, it's your fault."

Holly circled around Bobby and walked out to the outer office. Through the glass door she could see flashing lights and a crowd of people being held back by the police. She thought she also saw television cameras.

She picked up the phone and a voice immediately said, "We understand there's a terrorist in there with a weapon."

"Not exactly," said Holly.

"What'd he say?" asked Bobby from the doorway.

Holly put her hand over the mouthpiece. "He thinks you're a terrorist."

"Damn," muttered Bobby, butting his head against the wall.

"Are there more than one?" Holly was being asked.

"Sir, it isn't terrorists," she said. "It's only my ex-husband with a gun."

"What's your name, lady?"

Holly thought of her name appearing in the newspapers the next day. "I don't think my name is important. What you're doing out there is making a bad situation worse."

"What are his demands?"

"His demands?"

"Tell them I want a million dollars and a plane out of the country," said Bobby.

"Get serious," Holly shot back at him.

"What did he say?" asked the disembodied voice.

"He didn't say anything."

"I thought I heard a demand for a million dollars and a plane out of the country."

"He was just making a joke."

"Listen, lady, is there a guy with a gun in there or isn't there?"

"Yes, but I don't think it's loaded. I think he's bluffing."

Bobby, looking outraged, pointed the gun at the ceiling and blew a hole through it.

Holly dropped the phone on the floor.

"Pick it up," said Bobby.

"Pick it up yourself. What the hell do you think you're doing, Bobby? Those people out there aren't joking. You want to be killed, is that it?"

"I said pick up the phone."

Holly, who realized she had never really known her ex-husband, slowly leaned down and picked up the phone.

"Is there a casualty in there?" someone shouted in her ear.

"No. He was just proving his gun is loaded. He shot a hole in the ceiling."

"Let me talk to him."

"I don't think he'll come to the phone, not with you on the other side of the glass door."

"Tell him we want some pizza," said Bobby. "There's a Sal's Pizza in this shopping center, isn't there?"

"No pizza," said Holly. Ordering pizza would just be a delay, and she wanted this settled as quickly as possible. "What are your conditions, Bobby? What do I have to do to make you put down that gun and surrender to the police?"

"It's too late for that."

"It's not too late. It'll be too late when someone gets hurt, though."

"Hang up the phone."

Holly did what he said.

"Come on back in here. We're going to have us a hearing, just like I said."

Holly walked back into the meeting room as Sylvia was saying, "All right, so we can't have pizza. We could order in from a salad bar, couldn't we? None of us eat before we come here to weigh in, Holly, and stress causes hunger."

Maybe it did. Maybe that was why she continued to put on weight after her marriage. Right now, though, she wasn't hungry. Right now she was angry, which also caused stress, as did Bobby's gun. But stress wasn't always a bad thing. It usually made her mind work faster, and right now she needed it to work fast in order to figure out how to get everyone out of there without anyone getting hurt.

Holly saw that Bobby was removing his coat and carefully hanging it up. Bobby was a clothes fanatic: he loved to buy them, he loved to wear them, and taking good care of them always came before other considerations.

Beneath his coat he was wearing a black cashmere sweater with a gold chain showing in the V, form-fitting black wool trousers and black boots that had no doubt been recently polished but were now a little dirty from the slush in the streets. He was looking good enough for several of the female members to be giving him the once-over. Well, they were welcome to him. They would soon find that behind the good looks and the genial manner he assumed in public, he was the kind of man who treated his dog better than his woman.

Bobby, still carrying the gun, walked around the chairs and up to the podium. He smiled out at his audience. "What we're going to do is this. I'm going to tell you about my marriage, and then I'll open it up to questions and answers. After which Holly will get a shot at it. And when we're finished, we're going to take a little vote in here. That's all I ask from you. After we're finished you'll all be free to leave."

One of the women raised her hand and Bobby called on her.

"What about Christmas dinner?" she asked him.

"We're not going to be here that long," said Bobby.

The woman was shaking her head. "Holly was going to tell us what we could eat on Christmas."

Bobby looked a little exasperated. "I don't care what you eat, lady. Now could we get started or do you want to be here all night?"

"After this is over," Holly interjected, "we can continue with the Weight Watchers meeting."

"Not likely," said Arnold. "The police are going to want to take statements from all of us."

Sylvia asked, "Did you see any TV cameras out there, Holly?"

Holly nodded.

Bobby swung on her. "TV?"

"Yes, Bobby, you'll probably be on the eleven o'clock news."

Bobby's eyes began to light up.

Holly shook her head. "Is that the image you want as an Elvis Presley impersonator? They'll probably be calling you the Weight Watchers Terrorist."

Bobby, whose ambition had always been to get on television, didn't look as though he cared what got him on. He was smiling now, nodding his head, and as soon as he began to speak, she knew he was out to win friends and influence people.

Bobby folded his arms on the podium and leaned forward to talk to the people in a folksy manner. "Let me tell you folks about the first time I ever laid eyes on Holly...."

Holly sighed. Knowing Bobby's love of being center stage to a receptive audience, she was afraid it was going to be a very long night.

Interlude

She sat on the arm of the sofa and watched him as he read it. He was taking an awfully long time, going back to read some parts over and taking forever to get to the end. She hoped he wouldn't laugh at her attempt. She hadn't written anything since she was a kid when she had written out of unhappiness more than anything else, but she had always made good grades in English.

He finally turned over the last typewritten page and set the stack of paper on the coffee table.

She kept quiet as long as she could, which was about six seconds, and then she said, "Well?"

"I didn't know you were such a good typist, honey."

She punched him on the arm.

"I only saw a couple of typos."

"Will you please tell me what you think?"

"Well, I see one major problem."

She felt a sinking feeling and got up and walked across the room. It was awful; he hated it!

"The problem is, I'm never going to be able to do my chapters that well."

She turned around, a smile spreading across her face. "You thought it was okay?"

"I'm impressed," he said. "It reads like a real book."

"Are you serious? Do you really mean that?"

He held out his arms and she ran to the couch, throwing herself in his lap.

"That only took you a week?"

"Well, I spent hours on it."

"Maybe you should write the whole thing."

"No. I think we definitely need your viewpoint. Anyway, I don't think I could write a whole book by myself. Writing half of one doesn't sound as hard."

He hugged her close for a moment, and then said, "Can you take a little criticism?"

She thought about that for a moment. "A little."

"It was humorous. I mean, you're writing about a hostage situation, and I found it funny."

"I know. I realized that when I was writing it. But some of it was so ludicrous, you know?"

He nodded. "I thought it was funny when I first heard it on the news. The newscaster was trying to keep a straight face, but you could tell he wanted to laugh."

"It didn't seem all that funny at the time. I mean, there was Bobby with a gun, and that seemed serious, but then Arnold would say something, or someone would want to order pizza, and I'd want to laugh."

"Is it okay to have humor in these books?"

"Oh, sure. I always love it when they're humorous."

"Another thing. And I'm not criticizing you, honey, but you make yourself sound extremely cool and collected."

"I was."

"Yes, I know, but don't you think if some woman's ex-husband walks in with a gun she'd scream or cry or something?"

"Let's get one thing straight, darling. I do not like wimpy heroines. And since I wasn't wimpy in real life, I don't see why I have to make her wimpy."

"All right, I was only asking."

"Did I come across as a wimp on the news?"

He shook his head. "No, you came across as very much in control. I remember thinking that."

"You know something? This is really easy writing something that actually happened."

"I guess it's my turn now."

"Yes."

"I'm not sure I can write that well."

"Sure you can. I've read some of the things you've written."

"Do I get longer than a week?"

"No. I think we should stick to a schedule. Anyway, we ought to do it while it's still fresh in our minds."

"Did he really call you those names?"

She sat up a little and looked at him. "He certainly did. Do you think I'd make something like that up?"

"I could kill him for that."

"Oh, he's just ignorant, that's all. He's just the neighborhood bully who grew up and kept on picking on people who couldn't fight back. And I took it, which is even worse. If I'd liked myself at all in those days I would've just walked out."

"I wish I'd met you then. I would've taken you away from him fast enough."

She put her arm around his neck and leaned down so that their foreheads touched. "No, you wouldn't have. I was fat and miserable and the world's biggest martyr. You wouldn't have liked me."

"I think I would've."

"Well, much as I love you, what I needed at the time wasn't another man. I wasn't ready for a normal relationship until I began to like myself."

"Tell me something, how did it end that night? Did you put the vote to the meeting?"

She said, "It was unanimous. In my favor. I tell you, when that group got through with Bobby, he walked out of there a beaten man."

"I remember that's how he looked. I could almost feel sorry for him, losing you."

"He'd already lost me a long time before that night."

He said, "Do you have to go out tonight?"

"I have a Weight Watchers meeting."

"Great. Then I can sneak out to Burger King."

"Don't you dare! Anyway, I figure you can start working on the next chapter."

"Tonight?"

"You have anything better to do?"

"I thought I'd relax."

She got off the couch and then reached for his hands and pulled him up. "Go on—off to the typewriter. I can't wait to read your version of what happened."

Chapter Two

When the letters spelling out "NewsBreak" flashed across the screen, Tom, whose furnace didn't seem to be working properly, was wrapped in a plaid flannel comforter, his feet soaking in a bucket of hot water, watching the Knicks game. A newsbreak acted like a commercial for him, which meant getting up, heading quickly for the kitchen—and in some cases the john—and availing himself of another beer.

He had gotten as far as lifting his feet out of the hot water when he heard the words "hostage situation." Thinking it was another such episode in the Middle East, he untangled the comforter from himself and was walking by the TV screen on the way to the kitchen when he happened to glance down and saw that the video camera was panning the shopping center where he had his office.

He was freezing and his feet were in danger of acquiring icicles, but it wasn't every day he got free advertising on TV, especially during a Knicks game. Then he remembered the "hostage situation" part, which didn't scan. A hostage situation in Queens?

He decided to forgo the beer and headed back to the couch as the announcer said, "Just in, there is a hostage situation in progress at a Weight Watchers meeting in Rocky Inlet, Queens.''

Tom began to laugh. The announcer, who was not familiar to Tom, was trying very hard to keep a straight face. He was looking straight at the camera and his eyes were watering and his mouth was twitching as he said, ''We'll go now to Mary Ellison, who's on the scene. Mary?''

A good-looking black woman bundled up in a white furry coat was seen standing in the parking lot of Tom's neighborhood shopping center. Behind her he could clearly see the Chinese take-out place and his office. He was glad now he forfeited the extra money to Con Ed every month for leaving his sign on at night. Right now millions of people were seeing it.

''What we have here, Jim,'' the woman was saying into a microphone, ''is a hostage situation. It seems that forty minutes ago the police were alerted that a terrorist with a gun had taken a total Weight Watchers meeting hostage. As of right now, Queens police have the building surrounded and there is a SWAT team on the roof. The shopping center, which has a toy store, is teeming with Christmas shoppers, while inside the Weight Watchers offices a real-life drama is being played out.''

''Get back to the game,'' muttered Tom. The very people he hoped were seeing his sign would by now, he figured, prefer to return to the Knicks game.

The screen now showed the newscaster, who was promising to interrupt the game many more times that evening as the hostage situation developed.

Tom wasn't thrilled to hear that. It was bad enough they constantly interrupted for commercials. When the station, instead of going back to the game, went instead to a commercial, Tom got back up and headed for the kitchen. He got himself another Miller Lite, and while he was out there opened a new bag of potato chips. He also lit the two front burners of the gas stove, hoping the heat might find its way to the living room. First thing in the morning he was going to have to call someone to take a look at his furnace.

He got back to the living room just in time to see the beginning of a great lay-up, which wasn't brought to its natural conclusion because once more there was a news flash. Tom swore at the person responsible for depriving him of watching a basketball game in peace.

Mary in the white furry coat was now interviewing a woman in a red wool dress and no coat who must be freezing to death.

"Can you tell us what happened in there?" asked Mary.

The woman, shaking so hard from the cold she could barely speak, said, "Some crazy man came in waving a gun. At first I thought he was a member, but when I saw the gun I went screaming out of there."

"Did you notify the police?" asked Mary.

"I went right to the Chinese take-out place and they let me use their phone."

"Can you tell me how many hostages there are in there?"

"Twenty-two, including the leader."

Mary turned to the camera. "So far, Jim, there has been one gunshot reported."

"Can you talk to someone in charge?" Jim's voice was heard to ask.

"The rumor is that the terrorist has asked for a million dollars and a plane out of the country."

"He didn't look like a terrorist," said the woman who had reported the crime.

"Can you describe for us what he looked like?" asked Mary.

"Perfectly. He was about five foot eight, I couldn't tell his weight because he was warmly dressed, but he wasn't fat. I can always tell if someone is fat."

At that point, Tom picked up his remote control and turned to another channel. When the same thing was playing on every local channel, he turned off the set.

Maybe he ought to go down there and see what was happening. After all, it was only three blocks away, and the police couldn't keep him out of there because he had his office to protect. Right now there was probably a sharpshooter on the roof of his office just waiting for the opportunity to blow a hole through his roof.

And it couldn't be any colder out there than it was in his house.

He turned on the TV again to catch the score while he put on his socks and shoes. Instead of the game, though, there was a picture of an extremely fat woman holding up a picture in an ornate gold frame of a very fat young woman in a wedding dress. At first Tom thought it was a commercial, but then he heard the now-familiar voice of Jim saying, "And that was Mrs. Benson, the mother of the leader of the Weight Watchers meeting who is being held hostage. And now we'll return to our regularly scheduled programming."

The station immediately went to another commercial, and Tom gave it up and turned it back off. He also turned off the burners, and then put on his parka with the hood pulled up, found his fur-lined gloves and let himself out of the house.

He had planned on driving over to the shopping center, but it occurred to him that the police probably weren't letting any cars into the parking lot, so instead he walked.

Most of the houses on his block had Christmas lights and decorations. A couple of them had even gone overboard, with plastic Santas and reindeer spread across their lawns. He figured his neighbors probably thought he was Jewish. But then if he were Jewish, he'd at least have a menorah in the window. He didn't have anything. He had meant to get a tree, but kept putting it off and now it was really a little late. And if he got a tree he'd have to get lights and ornaments and all that other stuff.

He could at least get a wreath for his door. Last year, though, he had put a wreath on the door of his apartment and the next day it had been stolen. Too bad someone didn't steal those plastic Santa Clauses and reindeer.

He'd get a wreath. He'd definitely get a wreath. And maybe some branches to put on his mantel that would make the room smell good. Of course he could always buy some of that scented spray that would do the same thing.

Anyway, he wasn't a total Scrooge. He had gotten a tree for the office. Not that he probably would have thought of it himself, but his secretary had nagged him until he finally told her to go buy one and charge it to the office. That's what he could do. He could take the tree home from the office Christmas Eve. No sense in leaving it alone over the three-day weekend when he could be enjoying it.

He hadn't really liked Christmas since he was a kid. In those days his parents had put up a tree and taken him to see Santa Claus and it had been a real holiday. Ever since he and his brothers grew up, though, the entire family, with the exception of him, took off for one of the Caribbean islands for the holidays and their main purpose was to get a tan. He stayed home. He saw absolutely no reason to get a tan in the winter when the only parts of him that showed were his face and his hands when they weren't in gloves. Why should he burn his back and his chest and his legs just so that he could peel when he got back to the city?

When he got within a block of the shopping center he could see the commotion. First of all there was a huge traffic jam created by all the people trying to get into the parking lot to buy some last-minute toys and being denied entry by what looked like half the police in Queens. Then there were all the people either lured by the flashing lights or, like him, who, having seen it on TV, decided to walk over and take a first-hand look.

Tom didn't like people like that. They seemed to him to be the same kind of people who slowed down when they saw a traffic accident or followed fire engines to the scene of the fire. They were people who thrived on tragedy. He wasn't like that. He was just going to check on his office, make sure it was all right, and then he'd probably get a pizza and head back home to see the rest of the game.

When he got to the shopping center he saw that uniformed police had the center blocked off. Even the TV people weren't being allowed in. He walked purposely up to one of the officers, his wallet already out in case he was asked for ID, and said, "Sir, I have to get to my office in there."

"Move it, buddy," said the cop.

"I don't think you understand," said Tom. "My office happens to be in this shopping center and it's imperative that I get to it."

"You suicidal, buddy, or just plain stupid?"

Tom didn't like to misuse his power, but being polite wasn't getting him anywhere. "I happen to be an attorney, officer, and I believe I'm within my rights—"

"You want to be arrested for obstructing justice or do you want to move?"

"Sir—"

"You some ambulance chaser or what?"

Tom tried a smile. "If you'd just look over there for a minute, you see that flashing neon light?"

"You talking about that beer sign?"

"It's not a beer sign," said Tom. "It happens to say Law Office."

"You kidding me? In flashing *neon*?"

"Some people consider it innovative."

"I consider it a piece of garbage," said the cop.

"If I could just be allowed—"

"Buddy, would you just shut up? I got a job to do here and you're not making it any easier."

Tom decided he didn't like the officer's attitude. He'd run across his type in court, the type who always thought they knew everything. Instead of continuing the argument, he decided to walk down to the other end of the shopping center and see if he was allowed inside Sal's Pizza.

He passed by the newswoman he had seen on TV who was now interviewing the husband of one of the female hostages. He heard the husband say, "I knew nothing good was going to come of her going to those meetings," and then the woman interrupted him because someone was yelling through a bullhorn for the terrorist to give himself up.

Tom hoped he would. That way he could get a couple of slices of pizza and get home before the game was over. He watched the door to the Weight Watchers office for a minute, but didn't see a terrorist coming out with his hands in the air. When he looked higher and saw all the men with rifles on the tops of the buildings, he decided the terrorist wasn't so dumb. Tom wouldn't walk out into that, either.

And now he was sympathizing with the terrorist. He always sympathized with the underdog, though, and the terrorist seemed to have things stacked against him. What he was going to need if he got out of there alive was a good lawyer. Tom shook his head. Now he was beginning to *think* like an ambulance chaser.

He was close enough now to see into Sal's but the only person in the pizza shop was a cop guarding the door. The lights were on, the place looked open, but no one was doing business. He looked around the crowd to see if he could find Sal's bald head, but couldn't. But then who would be out in the cold without his head covered?

There was a large contingent of people in one group who were complaining about being evacuated from Toys Я Us. All the laser beam guns would be sold by the time they got back in the store.

Laser beam guns? For their kids? So that maybe they could grow up to be terrorists and hold a Weight Watchers meeting hostage? It was a crazy world.

It was also a cold world, at least this part of it, and he decided he had been wrong. It wasn't as cold in his house as it was outside. Furthermore, if he bought some wood he could make a fire and at least the living room would be warm. He could cross the street to the Safeway and buy some Presto Logs. And then he could carry them home three blocks.

It was a big decision. Would he rather freeze or would he rather have sore arms the next day?

TOM GOT THE FIRE LIT and then turned the game back on. He was able to watch two and a half consecutive minutes of play before the announcer was back on with recent developments in the hostage situation.

Tom pulled the couch closer to the fire, moved the TV set for a better angle, then got back under his comforter. The next thing he knew he was waking up and the game seemed to be over because the regular news broadcast was on. At least he'd be able to find out the final score.

Right in the middle of a story about another Queens politician being indicted, they switched again to on-the-scene coverage. "In a tense situation that has lasted the better part of three hours..." Tom was just about to switch it off out of frustration and go to bed when the camera went live to the scene and he saw about sixty cops converging on one lone man who was emerging from the Weight Watchers office.

The terrorist looked small and sad and alone. He also looked like just an average neighborhood guy. And then the terrorist spotted the TV cameras and put his arm up to cover his face. Tom, for some unaccountable reason, felt sorry for him.

The camera then switched to a group of women and one man, all overweight in varying degrees, before it zeroed in on a close-up of a slim young woman who was holding her arms up in the air like Rocky Balboa after a fight. She looked a little like Sissy Spacek, and Tom found himself thinking that if they made a movie about the hostage situation that was who should play her part.

He wondered who he'd cast as the terrorist. Someone ordinary, rather innocuous. Maybe Danny De-Vito. He was too old for the part, but he'd be funny. He'd love to see Danny DeVito playing a terrorist. He couldn't quite see a serious actress like Sissy Spacek making a movie with Danny DeVito, though.

Tom decided he'd ruined enough of his evening being manipulated by the news media and switched off the TV and decided to take a hot bath before going to bed. And tomorrow, first thing, he was going to buy a couple of space heaters in case his furnace ever acted up again.

TOM WAS IN HIS OFFICE working out the fine points of a will for one of his clients when Jolene, his secretary/receptionist/office manager, and anything else he could think of when he needed something done, buzzed him.

He picked up the phone. "Yes, Jolene?"

"There's someone out here who wants to see you."

Tom hoped it was a client, preferably one who didn't want a will drawn up. He had gotten a C in Wills in law school and had thought it the most boring course with the possible exception of Real Property. "Send him in," he told her.

"I'll send her in," said Jolene.

The last thing he had been expecting was the Sissy Spacek look-alike from TV the night before, but unless he was hallucinating, it was she. Although why she would need a lawyer unless she was going to sue the terrorist for something like mental distress was beyond him. As though the poor guy probably didn't have enough troubles.

"Have a seat," he told her.

She remained standing by the door. "Are you a criminal lawyer?" she asked him.

"I handle all kinds of cases. Would you like some coffee?"

"I need a criminal lawyer."

He couldn't have gotten it that mixed up, could he? Had she been the terrorist? No, not possible; she'd still be in jail. "My secretary could fix you some tea if you prefer."

"Do you know what caffeine does to your body?"

Actually, he knew exactly what it did: it kept him awake. "I guess I should say right up front that I saw you on TV last night. I still don't know who won the Knicks game."

"The Knicks lost."

Tom sighed, and was lost in contemplation of another losing season when he realized she was finally taking a seat in the leather chair facing his desk. She hadn't removed her pink down coat, though, as though ready to leave at a moment's notice if he didn't prove satisfactory.

"Did someone recommend me to you?"

"No. You look familiar, though. I think I've seen you around."

She looked familiar, too, but he was sure that was because she still looked like Sissy Spacek. Sandy hair, blue eyes, some freckles on her face. Younger, though, and even cuter. She didn't much look like someone in need of a criminal lawyer, but he had read somewhere that most criminals had blue eyes. Or maybe that was serial killers.

"How did you happen to hear about me?" he asked her, wondering if she had seen his latest ad in the Pennysaver. A few of his colleagues had been up front about telling him how tasteless they thought it was, but he had liked it. It had been humorous, a quality he found sadly lacking in the legal profession.

"I didn't hear about you," she said. "I keep seeing your sign flashing whenever I'm in the shopping center. I couldn't believe it the first time I saw it."

"I collect neon signs," said Tom, glancing around his office at several more strategically placed. "It looks great in here when it's dark out."

She looked less than certain of that and he contemplated drawing the blinds and turning on the signs, then thought better of it. He needed a case more than he needed a light show.

"So, you need a lawyer?" he asked her.

"I thought you said you saw me on TV."

"I did."

"Then why would you think I needed a lawyer?"

"I didn't get the impression you were the terrorist, but now you're in here looking for a criminal lawyer."

"He's not a terrorist."

"He didn't strike me as one, but that's what they were calling him on TV."

"I guess you didn't read the newspaper this morning."

"No."

"Well, the man who held us hostage . . . he's my ex-husband."

And who said the soap operas weren't like real life?

"Right before he gave himself up last night, he begged me to get him a lawyer. I wasn't going to. Actually, I figured he had a lot of nerve even asking me, but this morning I talked to his parents and they've washed their hands of him. They've had nothing but threatening phone calls and reporters at their door and they said Bobby could rot in jail as far as they were concerned."

"Do you know when he's going to be arraigned?"

"In an hour. You understand, I'm not hiring you, I'm just acting for Bobby. Anyway, I imagine I'll be testifying against him."

"Just for old times' sake?" He couldn't help it. He just couldn't take it seriously.

She gave him a dubious look. "Will you take the case or not?"

Was she kidding? He'd die for the case. "I'll go talk to him. If he wants to hire me, then fine."

She started to get up and he said, "Do you want to tell me about it?"

"As a state's witness, I don't think I should be talking to you."

The average person knew more about the law than he wished they knew. Probably from watching too much TV. "Well, just one more question then. What's Bobby's full name?"

"Robert McKiever."

"And your name?"

"Holly Benson."

"You remarried?"

She looked like she was about to walk out, but then she said, "Benson was my maiden name. I took it back legally."

"Well, perhaps I'll see you in court, Ms. Benson."

"Probably sooner than you think," she said as she walked out of his office.

He hated that. He really hated it when someone got in a parting shot like that. He was sure it was supposed to sound mysterious, but he was damned if he was going to let it bug him.

As soon as he heard the outer door close, Jolene came into his office. She was looking as smug as a cat with a mouse's tail hanging out of its mouth. "Do you know who that was?" she asked him.

He nodded. "I saw her on TV last night."

"I missed that," said Jolene. "I was Christmas shopping last night. But she's on page three of the *News* this morning."

"Does she remind you of anyone?"

"Who?"

"That's what I'm asking you."

"I don't think so."

"She asked me to defend her ex-husband, last night's terrorist."

Jolene became even more animated. "Are you going to?"

"Hell yes, if he wants me. A case like that could be great for business."

"You know who he is?"

"Robert McKiever."

"You ever go to the Skylark Lounge?"

"Over by K mart?"

She nodded.

"No, I've never been in there."

"Well, he does an Elvis Presley act there on Saturday nights. He is so good you would swear Elvis came back from the dead."

What a terrible thought. He couldn't think of a whole lot of people he'd less like see come back from the dead. "You're an admirer of his?"

Jolene blushed. "Would you get me his autograph?"

"You can get one yourself. If I take his case you'll probably be seeing a lot of him. Unless the judge sets such a high bail he doesn't get out, which could happen if the press insists on calling him a terrorist."

"I thought it was romantic," said Jolene.

"I know there must be some women who find terrorism romantic, Jolene, but I hadn't thought you'd be one of them."

"I never said I found terrorism romantic. But the paper says he held the Weight Watchers meeting hostage in an effort to win back his wife."

"His ex-wife."

"Whatever. I think that's romantic. If some guy did that for me, I'd run back to him in a minute. Particularly if he was an Elvis impersonator."

And this was the young woman who was so intelligent he was trying to persuade her to go to law school? He'd have to do a little rethinking on that subject.

"Well, I'm going to go over to the jail and see if I can see him before the arraignment," said Tom.

"You want me to go with you?"

"No, Jolene, I want you to stay in the office and answer the phone and open the mail and type up the will I just dictated."

"When will you be back?"

"I should be back in time for lunch. Order me in a pizza from Sal's, will you?" He'd been dying for one ever since he'd been deprived the night before.

Maybe the terrorist would be out of jail by then and they could share it.

Interlude

"Well," she said, looking secretly pleased about something.

He waited, and when she didn't say anything else, he said, "So? What do you think?"

"Sissy Spacek? You really thought I looked like Sissy Spacek?"

"I still do."

"I don't look anything like Sissy Spacek."

"I think you do. You're the same coloring and you both have that kind of innocent look about you. Those big eyes and that turned-up nose and those freckles."

"It sounded as though you were more interested in the basketball game."

"I was."

She flipped through the pages, found what she was looking for and read it again. "I see you felt sorry for Bobby."

He said, "I think we ought to get one thing straight."

"It sounds as though you sympathized with him."

"Look, honey, do you want me to write the truth as I remember it or do you want me to romanticize it out of all proportion?"

"I just don't see how you could sympathize with a terrorist."

"You *know* he wasn't a terrorist. Anyway, it's hard not to sympathize with the underdog, and when he walked out of there into the waiting arms of all those cops—"

"Yes, all right, maybe then. But what about inside when he held a gun on innocent Weight Watchers members?"

"But they didn't show that part on television. I can only go by what I saw. But if you want me to romanticize it, I can always write about how I fell madly in love with you the moment I saw you on TV."

"Did you?"

"No. But if it makes you happy, I can say I did."

"Did you fall madly in love with me when I walked into your office?"

He chuckled. "I wish I could say I did, but if you want me to be honest—"

"I don't necessarily want you to be honest."

He started to laugh. "Did you fall in love with me the moment you walked into my office?"

"Well, no, but I had other things on my mind."

"I was attracted, though."

"Because I looked like Sissy Spacek. If the real Sissy Spacek had walked into your office you would've fallen madly in love."

"That's not true."

"Tell me, why did you take the case? Was it because of me?"

He wasn't sure how to answer. If he told the truth, there was going to be trouble. He decided not to answer at all.

"All right, I know it wasn't because of me. It was because you sympathized with Bobby, right? You wanted to defend the underdog."

"Actually, that wasn't why I took it, either."

"No? Well, why did you take it?"

"I figured it was my big chance to get into criminal law. Not having any underworld connections, I wasn't getting any cases except for the occasional shoplifter. And I knew this one was going to get lots of publicity—"

"And you were going to get famous off me and Bobby."

"I'm not that mercenary. It's not every day that we have a hostage crisis in Queens, though."

"Well, I guess I can't tell you how to write your chapters."

"Look, I'll willingly concede that you're the writer and let you write the entire book if you want."

She was quiet for a moment, and then she moved over to the couch and sat beside him. He had a feeling she was going to break it to him gently that he couldn't write worth a damn, and he found, to his surprise, that he cared. He had enjoyed writing his chapter and he thought it was a good idea to get both viewpoints in the book. If he left it up to her it was bound to be hopelessly romanticized.

She leaned her head into his shoulder and he shifted his arm around her. "You know what?" she asked him.

"I know. I can't write. It sounded too factual, right? I had the feeling when I was writing it that it sounded like a news release."

"I hate to admit it, but I think you write much better than I do. It really moved along and held my interest."

"Did it sound like one of those books you read?"

"Not exactly, but I think that's okay. It sounded like a real man's point of view, which is kind of hard for a woman to do."

"I can always rewrite it, change a few things."

"I would have liked you to describe your house a little more."

"My *house*?"

"Yes."

"Who cares about my house? There's a hostage situation going on and you want me to describe my house?"

"Your house tells me something about you."

He said, "Oh, no, on this we're going to disagree. Watching the basketball game tells something about me. Walking over to the shopping center tells something about me. Not having Christmas decorations even tells something about me, although to tell you the truth, I thought of lying about that. I didn't want to come across as some kind of Scrooge. And I did mention my collection of neon lights. Anyway, to have described my house would've slowed down the plot."

"I think that flashing neon light in your office window tells a lot about you, but not the right thing. I have to admit that I was sure a lawyer with a flashing neon light would be just the kind of sleazy lawyer who would be perfect for Bobby."

"You thought my neon light was sleazy?"

"It's not exactly understated. I fully expected you to be wearing a plaid jacket and a flowered tie and a pinky ring with a big fake diamond."

"I must have been a real disappointment to you."

"Now that I know you, it fits. But at the time I thought a flashing neon sign was a bit suspect."

"We're not talking Wall Street here, or even Madison Avenue. I'm a storefront lawyer in a shopping center in Queens and I wanted to attract a criminal clientele."

"Plus you're crazy about neon."

"That too."

She said, "I think we should be proud of ourselves. We said we were going to do it and we already have two chapters completed. That's something, don't you think?"

"It's more fun than writing briefs."

"Well, maybe we'll be vastly successful and you won't have to be a lawyer anymore."

"Then I can be a stand-up comic."

"I meant we could be writers."

"Would you want to do it all the time?"

She thought about that for a moment. "No, I don't think so. I like getting out and meeting people. And if all we did was stay home and write, what would we find to write about?"

"So what are you going to put in the next chapter?" he asked her.

"I'm not sure. I was thinking maybe I should write a flashback and tell the story of my life. How I met Bobby and all that."

"And then the next chapter I'd tell the story of *my* life?"

"I don't think your life is important to the story."

"Not any of it?"

"Well, maybe bits and pieces. But not a whole chapter."

"I don't think you should do an entire chapter about your life, either. If I was reading it, I would want to know what happened next. I think you should just tell about your life in little segments throughout the book."

"The thing is, what came next was the arraignment and I wasn't there for that."

"It wasn't all that interesting. About all that happened was that the judge set bail at fifty thousand, which at the time I thought meant my client would be sitting it out in a cell."

"Not knowing about me."

"Right."

"Not yet knowing how resourceful I am."

"You're resourceful all right," he said, pulling her over on his lap. "You're constantly surprising me."

"But I'll bet you wouldn't have guessed what I did for a living when I walked into your office."

"Shhh," he said, tracing her lips with is finger.

She rubbed her nose against his chest. "Are we going to talk about the book or what?"

"Or what," he decided, leaning down to kiss her. It was his expert opinion that they had talked about the book enough. Now it was time to move ahead to more interesting possibilities.

For once she didn't give him an argument.

Chapter Three

If the location of Benson Bail Bond looked more like a used car lot than anything else, it was because Holly took in more cars than money.

As a bail bondsperson, she didn't have connections. She didn't get drug dealers with ready, if suspect, cash for their associates; Benson obviously didn't sound Italian so the mob lawyers went elsewhere. The kind of clientele Benson Bail Bond attracted were the down-and-outers, the husbands and wives and families who could barely scrape together the ten percent necessary to bail out their errant loved ones and who usually used the barter system instead.

Holly's bail bond business was housed in a twelve-by-twelve-foot frame building set on concrete blocks, located on a half acre of not-so-prime property in Rocky Inlet. The property could almost be called swampy except that there weren't any swamps in Queens. The best thing about the location was that it was conveniently close to the jail.

There was a businesslike sign on the roof of the building that said Benson Bail Bond. When she took over the business, she made the sign a little less businesslike by the addition of some painted daisies in yellow and white. She thought it softened the effect, made it look less like a place that dealt exclusively with people who were in trouble with the law. Her female customers often remarked on the sign, saying how much they liked it; her male customers generally ignored it.

The building inside was one large room. There were two long neon light fixtures suspended from the ceiling that turned anyone under them the color of a corpse. There was a large oak desk that had been considered a cheap piece of used furniture when her father first bought it but now could probably be considered a halfway valuable antique. Behind the desk was an oversize swivel chair, also in oak, which her father had had custom made to fit his proportions and which Holly now felt lost in. There was an entire wall of four-drawer metal file cabinets that had been painted black at one time and were now peeling in some places. There was a clock on one wall and a wall calendar advertising Holly's bank on another. There were two gray metal folding chairs facing Holly's desk where her customers sat. There was a card table set up with a coffeepot and Styrofoam cups and a bowl full of packets of artificial sweetener. In one corner was Holly's most recent addition, a Christmas tree decorated entirely in white lights, silver balls and lots of tinsel. It sparkled and caught the light and generally brightened up the office.

Holly had had to restrain herself from fixing up the office. She knew her taste ran to flowered chintz and framed pastels on the walls and she also knew this kind of decor wouldn't go over with her customers. A bail bond office was not supposed to look like a boudoir; it was supposed to look like serious business.

What the office didn't have was toilet facilities, which meant that when Holly felt the need for such, she had to switch on the answering machine, lock up the office and head for her trailer, which was across the lot and under the one tree. In between the office and her trailer were numerous cars in various stages of disrepair. There was also a rowboat, almost hidden by the snow; a Honda motorcycle with two flat tires; and an electric golf cart with a tarp protecting it from the elements.

The day after the hostage situation, as soon as Holly had interested Tom Cunningham in taking Billy's case, she headed for work.

She had a feeling Bobby wasn't going to be pleased with her choice of a lawyer. Bobby would be happier with a lawyer of the sort Holly had expected Tom to be. Bobby's considered opinion of lawyers was that they were sleazy con men at best and he would have been happier to have an attorney who was just that. The unexpected was going to throw him.

Tom Cunningham had been the unexpected. If Holly had had to describe Tom to someone, she would have said this: picture a rangy outfielder, one with long legs and long arms, the kind who looked like he would trip over his own feet but who, when in action, moved with grace. Picture him with blond hair, a little long so that it curled down from beneath his baseball cap and covered his neck. Picture faded blue eyes that almost disappeared when he smiled. Picture a slightly bent nose and a wide mouth that curved up in a smile even when he wasn't smiling. Picture all this and then dress him up in a dark blue suit with a white shirt and a tie that was already pulled loose at nine o'clock in the morning. Then ask, "What is wrong with this picture?"

Or, for instant recognition, picture Jeff Bridges a few years younger and a few pounds lighter. Only she never would have thought of casting Jeff Bridges as a lawyer. A baseball player, yes; an attorney, no. She would have loved to be there when Tom and Bobby met. They were about as different as any two men she ever met.

Holly saw the television reporters as soon as she pulled up in front of her office. They had to be television reporters; clients didn't generally videotape their transactions with her. She debated whether she should continue driving and avoid them, but that wasn't any way to conduct a business. A client might need her services desperately, as desperately as she needed their business.

Everyone had called her last night to say they had seen her on television. She had been embarrassed at first, even more embarrassed when she heard her mother had been on, too, holding up Holly's old wedding picture for everyone to see. When she had talked to her mother, her mother hadn't seen anything wrong with that. She had been thrilled for all her friends to see her capitalizing on her daughter being in a hostage situation.

Holly decided that no matter what they asked her, she would say, "No comment." People said that to reporters all the time and they almost seemed to expect it. She would be friendly, smile at them—and at the cameras—but she wouldn't answer any questions. Anything said now might prejudice Bobby's case and she didn't want to see him get off on some technicality like her mouthing off and all the prospective jurors hearing her and making up their minds in advance.

She hated it. She had never liked having her picture taken, even though these days she was somewhat more photogenic. She didn't like people she didn't know knowing who she was. She particularly didn't like the whole world knowing she had once been fat. Weight Watchers members were okay. After all, they had the same problem. But the other half of the world, the half who had always been thin, didn't need to know about it. It made her feel like some kind of freak.

She got out of the car and locked it and there was an instant surge from the crowd in her direction. She heard, "How are you feeling today, Holly?" and "Have you seen Bobby yet?" and "What were you feeling when your ex-husband was holding you hostage?" and a lot of other things that she didn't hear as clearly. They were being very familiar, calling her by her first name and acting like they were old friends, and she didn't like it a bit.

"No comment," she mumbled, forgetting to smile, trying to get by them, but they blocked her way and cameras were practically shoved in her face.

Holly pasted a patient smile on her face and stood there, waiting for them to let her through to the door of her office.

"We'd like to hear the story in your own words," said one of the female reporters, shoving a microphone within an inch of Holly's mouth.

Holly backed up a step. "I really have no comment to make," she told the reporter.

"Holly, honey, you're news," said one of the male reporters. "You're today's hot story."

"I'm sorry," said Holly.

"Your mother said she was sure there'd be a reconciliation between you and Bobby," said one of the
reporters. "Would you like to comment on that?"

She'd like to all right, but she wouldn't. She'd like
to tell them that her mother was crazy, that there was
zero possibility of her going back to Bobby, but she
didn't want to see herself saying that on the news. She
didn't want to see herself saying *anything* on the news.

"If you'll excuse me, I have to open my office," she
told them, trying to squeeze by a burly man with a
video camera on his shoulder.

They finally parted a little and she was able to get by
them, and as she approached the door to her office she
heard one of them saying, "That was Holly Benson,
the heroine of last night's hostage situation in Rocky
Inlet."

She was inserting the key in the door when there was
a tentative tap on her shoulder. She turned around to
see a weasel-faced man with a red stocking cap pulled
past his eyebrows.

"I said I had no comment," said Holly.

"I'm authorized to pay you up to ten thousand
dollars for an exclusive," he said, his eyes almost
lighting up when he named the figure.

"Are you serious?"

"Perfectly serious."

For a moment she thought of what she could do
with ten thousand dollars. "What newspaper?" she
asked him.

"The *Investigator*," he said, in the same tone of
voice that someone else would use to say the *Times*.
She thought he had guts. Holly wouldn't be caught
dead buying the *Investigator*, let alone admit to
working for them.

"I have no respect for that paper," said Holly.

"Look at it this way," said the reporter. "I'm going to do a story about you either way. You can do it your way and get paid for it, or I'll do it my way and you won't see a cent out of it."

"Does that seem ethical to you?" asked Holly.

"What's ethics got to do with it?"

Holly shook her head. "Sorry, I still have no comment." She turned the key in the lock and pushed open the door. When he tried to follow her in, she said, "If you continue to harass me, I'll have to call the police."

He handed her a card. "If you change your mind, give me a call. Maybe I can get them up to fifteen."

Holly slammed the door in his face. It wasn't right. She had to work very hard, sometimes night and day for months and months, to make fifteen thousand dollars. And yet some tabloid was willing to pay her that much just to get her to shoot off her mouth about her personal business for a few minutes. But it wasn't the newspaper's fault. It was the fault of the kind of nosy people out there who would pay good money to read such nonsense.

She turned on the electric heater by her desk before taking off her coat and muffler and boots and legwarmers. The light on the answering machine was blinking and she sat down at the desk and got a pen in readiness to take down her messages.

The first one was from her mother, saying, "Pick up, Holly, I know you're there." Pause. "Don't think you're fooling me for one minute, young lady. If you think I'm going to talk to all these reporters all by myself, you have another think coming." There was a longer pause, and then the sound of a phone being forcefully hung up.

Holly craved a quick dose of sugar. Her mother always affected her that way. Since she couldn't have sugar, because she was a reformed sugarholic, phony sugar would have to do and she got up and plugged in the coffeepot. She couldn't even wait long enough to make a new pot; yesterday's decaffeinated would have to do.

The second message was from a reporter, and as soon as he had identified himself, Holly fast-forwarded the machine to the third message.

"Holly?" she heard. "This is Dugan at the jail. God, I hate these machines. Hey, we have your ex down here and he's yelling for you. Want to give me a call?"

The fourth through seventh messages were also from reporters. The eighth was a recap from her mother. The ninth was a hang-up and that was it. Not one call from a prospective client.

She poured herself a cup of almost-hot coffee and sat back down at the desk. She tried to tell herself that there was sugar in the coffee, not Equal, but she wasn't fooled. It didn't taste bad, but it didn't give her a sudden surge of energy, either.

She dialed the jail, asked for Dugan, and when he came on, she said, "Hi, it's Holly. I got your message."

"You want the good news or the bad?"

"What good news? If you're talking about Bobby, there's no way it could be good."

There was a pause, then, "Actually, I was."

"Good? You must be the only one in town not calling him a terrorist."

Dugan laughed. "I don't know about being a terrorist, but he's sure as hell a terror."

"So what's the good news?"

"The lawyer you sent over. Cunningham. Bobby hired him on."

"Yeah, that's good. So, has he been arraigned yet?"

"They're up there now."

"What's the word on bail?"

"We weren't figuring on it, but with a good lawyer, who knows? Personally, I'm hoping he gets it. Another shift with him around and I'll quit the force."

"I hesitate to ask what the bad news is."

"I hate to be the one to tell you this, Holly, but Psycho jumped bail.'"

"Sykol," Holly automatically corrected him before the meaning sunk in. "No. Tell me you're kidding."

"I kid you not."

"Leaving me with a nine thousand dollar debt. Beautiful." It was enough to send her to the nearest bakery to pig out. Not only was she out the ten percent of the bail money that was hers to keep as the bail bond fee, but now she was also out the other nine thousand she had put up for the bond.

"You want me to call you and let you know if bail's set on Bobby?"

"I don't think I could take any more good news today."

"I'll let you know anyway."

She disconnected the call and then left the phone off the hook. With the way the day was going she didn't think she wanted to hear what happened next. Along with everything else, it was now bounty hunter time. She'd be damned if she was going to let Sykol leaving her holding the bag. No way. She'd find him if it took another nine thousand dollars to do it. The ironic thing about it was that Sykol got busted for printing money. She could use a little of that herself right about now.

An hour later she had an estimate on paper on how much available cash she could lay her hands on. Even assuming she could sell the golf cart in a community without a golf course in the middle of winter, it wasn't going to be enough to pay off the nine thousand and also meet her expenses. She either needed a lot of new business fast or she had to find Sykol. Or she could always prostitute herself and give that questionable reporter a call.

The only good news was that business should pick up over the holidays. Christmas was always good for domestic killings; New Year's excellent for fights in bars and drunks causing accidents. Toy stores weren't the only ones to cash in at Christmas.

She hadn't heard a car pull up, and the door opening surprised her. She heard "Holly," and looked up, and the good news was it wasn't a reporter.

The bad news was it was Flannery, Bobby's agent and not one of her favorite people.

"Hey, Flan," she said. "How's business?"

"Why the hell's your phone off the hook?"

"Reporters."

Flannery availed himself of a cup of coffee. As soon as he tasted it he was going to be sorry. "You should thank your lucky stars for all those reporters," said Flannery. The first sip of the coffee lessened his genial expression.

"I suppose you heard about Bobby."

"I'm here to bail him out. He said to throw the business your way."

"I don't know that I trust him not to jump bail," said Holly. "We're talking big-time here, Flan. We're talking terrorism."

"You got the first part of that right," said Flannery. "And I think I'll be keeping him too busy to jump bail. You know what Bobby is, Holly? He's a celebrity, in capital letters."

"You going to put him in a ski mask and let him sing revolutionary songs?"

"I got clubs wanting to book him as far away as Wilmington, Delaware."

"I hope this wasn't a publicity stunt, Flan."

"What're you talking about? You think holding a group of fat women hostage is good publicity?"

"I wouldn't have thought so, but I guess it was. Hell, some newspaper reporter was willing to pay me ten thousand for my story."

Flannery got a crafty look on his face. "What you need, kid, is an agent."

"Wrong, Flan, what I need is some business, and I guess I won't pass up yours. What kind of bail was set?"

"High, but I can make it. I figure it's a good investment. Fifty thousand."

"And you can always advertise Bobby as the fifty-thousand-dollar terrorist."

"Not bad," said Flannery.

Holly got out the form and passed it over to Flan to fill out. "You writing me a check, Flan?"

"Since I don't happen to have five thou on me."

The five thousand would considerably improve her financial situation. Which was the first time in history Bobby had been directly responsible for doing anything along those lines.

When Flan had written her out a check, Holly immediately filled out a deposit slip, then put them both in her bag. "You going to jail with me?" she asked Flan.

"I got business to do. Just be sure to tell him to give me a call."

Holly switched on the answering machine before locking up the office, then chose a vintage VW with a flower painted on its side to drive over to the jail. It had no shocks to speak of and it barely made it up a hill anymore, but there weren't any hills in Queens and she still thought it was the only car ever made that had any personality to it.

Dugan was at the desk when she got there and she handed over the form to him. "Bobby ready to go?" she asked.

"Bobby is more than ready," said Dugan with a grin. "In fact his cellmates are ready to break him out themselves just to get rid of him."

"Bobby being obnoxious?"

"Oh, no, not obnoxious. Bobby is being cute. Bobby has been doing Elvis for them and they're ready to cut out his tongue."

When Bobby was brought out he looked considerably more cheerful than when she had seen him last. "Hey, Holly, thanks for coming by," he said, as though he hadn't held a gun on her the night before.

"I'd like to give you a kick where you'd remember it the most," said Holly, keeping her distance from him.

"Hey, you gonna hold last night against me?" Bobby made as if to give her a hug, but she evaded him.

Dugan said, "How about you move your domestic quarrel out of the jail?"

"There's nothing domestic about it," said Holly, but she followed Bobby out of the door and into the parking lot.

"You going to give me a ride?" asked Bobby.

"Call a taxi."

"So okay, you're going to be difficult, I can live with that. At least drop me at a subway stop."

"Get your lawyer to give you a ride."

"Hey, I forgot to thank you for that. The guy's okay. Where'd you find him?"

"Did you happen to notice, while on your terrorist quest last night, a law office in the shopping center with a flashing neon light?"

"No, but I guess my mind was on other things."

"Like holding a gun on countless innocent people."

"Look, I don't even feel like riding with you if you're going to take that kind of an attitude," said Bobby.

"Good," said Holly, getting into her car and locking the door before Bobby could make his move. Let him walk home. She had done all for him that she planned on doing. He was acting as if what he did last night was no more serious than the time he let off the firecrackers in the boy's bathroom in high school.

Holly drove by her mother's house, saw a Channel Six van parked out in front, and kept driving. In the interests of harmony in the family, she decided not to even watch the news for the next few days.

She had been going to the same bank several times a week for the past two years, and today was the first day she was recognized and greeted by name. The power of the media was frightening. Even the bank manager came out and said good morning to her.

"I was thinking of joining Weight Watchers myself," the teller told her, causing Holly to take a second look at the young woman. As far as Holly could see she looked anorexic.

"You have to be overweight to join," said Holly.

"I feel so fat," said the woman, glancing down at her emaciated body.

Holly felt no sympathy. Thin people who felt fat needed a shrink, not consoling.

The woman slid the deposit receipt toward Holly, saying, "I saw your husband once at the Skylark. I could've died when he sang 'Love Me Tender.'"

"Ex-husband," Holly corrected her.

Holly left the bank, walked past a bakery where the smell of freshly baked bread gave her only minor heart palpitations, then walked into a drugstore and without even allowing her mind to know what she was doing, bought a pack of M&M candies. She ripped it open before she had even paid for it and popped two in her mouth. There had been a time when she would've popped the entire contents of the packet in her mouth, but even though she was falling by the wayside, she wasn't that far gone yet.

By the time she had paid for them and walked out of the store, remorse was setting in. How stupid it was to let Bobby drive her to eating candy. Two tiny little M&M candies weren't going to do serious damage to her weight loss, but then that was probably what alcoholics told themselves about the first drink.

She passed a trash can and told herself to throw the rest of them away. She couldn't do it. The idea of throwing something so deliciously edible away was too much for her. She would put them in her bag in case of an emergency and forget all about them.

Two more found their way into her mouth almost as though they had jumped in without benefit of her help. She let them slowly settle onto her tongue as the chocolate began to melt. She refused to bite into them. Biting into them was the way she really liked to eat them and she wouldn't allow herself that pleasure. She might be getting the taste, but she wasn't going to let herself get the crunch.

By the time she reached her car the packet was empty and she was feeling serious guilt. Never mind that she had told countless Weight Watchers groups that if they binged, not to feel guilty, just to get back on the program. It was simply impossible not to feel guilt. Especially when what she wanted most in the world was to turn around and go back to the drugstore for more.

What she needed was a Weight Watchers meeting, but it was almost two hours before there would be one to attend. She thought of driving by her mother's again. Seeing the rolls of fat on her mother always strengthened her resolve never to be obese again, but if she saw the Channel Six van there again she was sure the sight of it would send her back for more sweets.

She'd check out Sykol's house. Maybe he had skipped bail but not town. Getting him back in custody was worth any amount of candy.

She was standing by her car when she noticed a small group of people watching her. She stared at them while they stared at her, and then she heard the words "hostage situation" and she quickly unlocked her car and got inside. She would never be able to understand how Bobby thrived on this kind of attention. He liked nothing more than to be stared at. It was creepy.

She drove out to Far Rockaway and when she had found Sykol's address, it turned out to be a very small beach cottage that appeared to be boarded up.

She banged on the front door but there was no answer. Walking around the side of the house she saw that a window in the rear was broken, but when she peered inside, the house looked abandoned.

The cottage was one in a row of beach cottages, and every one but Sykol's had a sign warning of a guard dog. They weren't the kind of cheap people who bought signs but didn't buy dogs, either. She counted three Dobermans and two pit bulls before she decided it wasn't the kind of place where she'd want to hang out.

She knocked on some doors but either the people didn't know Sykol or, if they did, said they hadn't seen him around in a few weeks.

There was one nosy old lady who was more helpful. She told Holly she had seen Sykol loading up his car in the middle of the night and taking off.

"Do you know if he owns the cottage?" Holly asked her, thinking it wouldn't be the worst thing in the world if she got a beach cottage out of it. She didn't think she'd want to live in it, but she could always rent it out.

The old lady shook her head. "None of us own them. We all rent from the same man, some slum landlord who shows up once a month in his Mercedes to collect the rent, but never shows up if something goes wrong."

So much for her own summer house.

She made it back to Rocky Inlet in time to catch the noon Weight Watchers meeting.

"Well, if it isn't our celebrity," said Coralee, who was manning the desk.

"Don't remind me," said Holly.

"Business has picked up," said Coralee. "There were a lot of people who saw that 'before' picture of you on TV last night, and then saw the new, slim you walking out of the building and were impressed."

Holly weighed in, saw that instead of instantly gaining weight from the M&M candies, she had instead dropped half a pound, probably from not eating the night before. This cheered her up enough that she considered skipping the meeting and getting lunch instead, but the leader, Manny, caught sight of her and wanted her to tell him all about the night before, and she ended up attending the meeting and then having a salad with Manny afterward.

By the time she got back to the office, the day was pretty much shot. She ran through her phone messages and they were all from either her mother or reporters with one from the lawyer she had hired for Bobby.

Assuming it was business, she phoned Tom Cunningham. "This is Holly Benson. What's up?" she asked when he answered.

"I understand you bailed him out."

"His manager bailed him out. I'm just the bail bondsperson."

There was a lengthy silence, then, "I know. I couldn't believe your message when I called. I thought maybe it was a put-on."

"Listen, it's a business, even if I'm not exactly ready to retire on the profits."

"You get criminals out of jail for a living?"

"Isn't that what you do?"

"You just don't look the type."

"You don't look like a lawyer, either," countered Holly.

"Now that we've complimented each other, how about having dinner with me tonight?"

"Is this business?" asked Holly. "Because I don't think I should be discussing the case with you."

"No business, just dinner."

Dates weren't so easy to get that she turned them down lightly. Particularly when they were offered by honest citizens and not the dregs she bailed out of jail.

"Do you need some time to think about it?" he asked.

"No, dinner sounds fine," said Holly.

"Pick you up about six?"

"Great."

"Just one thing, I don't know where you live."

"Then how did you get my phone number?"

"Weight Watchers gave it to me. Only after I explained it had to do with the case, though."

"You know the bail bond place on Dycker Avenue?"

"The one with the flowers on the sign?"

"Some of us can't afford neon."

"Is that where you want me to pick you up?"

"That's where I live. In the trailer under the tree."

"You're sounding more and more intriguing. I don't believe I've ever dated a bail bondsperson who lived in a trailer beneath a tree."

"I've never dated a lawyer defending my ex-husband for terrorism, either. By the way, what was the charge?"

"I thought you didn't want to discuss the case?"

"I'm sure I'm the only one who doesn't know by now."

"There are multiple charges, the least of which was unlawful possession of a firearm and the worst being holding the people hostage."

"Well, good luck."

"That's very generous of you."

"I was kidding."

"I know. See you at six."

Holly wondered what Bobby would say if he knew his little stunt was directly responsible for her first date in three months.

She only hoped the date turned out to be worth it.

Interlude

He hadn't read more than two pages of her chapter
when he got a legal pad and a pen and started to take
notes. That made her so nervous she left the room and
went into the kitchen, but seeing his junk food occu-
pying most of the counter space made her even more
nervous, so she went back into the living room and sat
as far away from him as possible.

Maybe she was misjudging the situation. Maybe he
wasn't critiquing her work; perhaps, instead, he was
making notes on what he planned on writing next.

All right, so it wasn't a great chapter. She guessed
it could even be called boring. But there had been a lot
of stuff she needed to get in before moving on to the
interesting parts. One of those interesting parts being
their first date. Which, of course, he would now get to
write, which didn't seem fair. But she was rather interested in seeing his version of it.

She watched him pause in his reading and scribble
furiously on the legal pad. It was starting to bother
her. Actually, more than the writing was starting to
bother her. There was also the bowl of buttered popcorn sitting in front of him on the coffee table, to say
nothing of the empty beer cans, the bowl of bar nuts,

the half-eaten bag of barbecue potato chips and the Snickers bars sticking out of his pocket. He was a walking advertisement for junk food and it was starting to get to her.

No sooner had she thought that, when he absent-mindedly reached into his pocket, ripped the paper off the end of a candy bar and took a bite. He chewed it as though it was the most natural thing in the world. Which, she guessed, for him it was. Right now, at this very instant, she could easily cross the distance between them, choke him to death, eat the rest of the candy bar and have no qualms about it.

He sensed her watching him and looked up from his reading. "What's the matter?" he asked her.

"Nothing."

"Why are you staring at me like that?"

"I was just waiting for you to finish, that's all."

"I'll just be a few more minutes. Want to get me another beer?"

"No!" she found herself shouting, then forced herself to relax when she saw the look on his face. "Sorry, I'm just a little nervous, that's all."

"About what?"

"About all those notes you're making."

"Hey, don't worry, it's pretty good."

Pretty good? Hadn't he thought the last one was great?

She went out to the kitchen and opened him another beer. While she was there, she got herself a Diet Pepsi. She knew that someday she would stop missing sugar in drinks, but that day hadn't as yet arrived.

When she got back he was still making notes and she felt a sudden urge to pour the beer over his head, but she resisted and placed it on the coffee table instead.

"Are you almost finished?" she asked him.

"One more page."

She sat quietly, biting her fingernails, because if she didn't bite her fingernails she would be all over those potato chips in about another ten seconds. She tried to remember what it was she loved about him, but couldn't come up with a thing. Why couldn't she have fallen in love with a health nut who ate nothing but raisins and grains? She never was tempted by health food. Why did he have to be a junk-food junkie? Was she going to spend the rest of her life being tormented by the sight of him stuffing delectables into his mouth? Maybe there were worse things than being called Moose. Things like slow torture.

"Okay," he said, putting down the last page and settling back on the couch.

"Well?"

"I'm impressed you wrote this so quickly."

"I did it too quickly, didn't I? I should have taken more time."

"Not at all, it's got some good things in it."

She waited to hear what the good things were, but when they weren't forthcoming, she chewed on her nails some more.

"You want to discuss the notes I made?" he asked her.

"I guess so."

"First of all, I think the description of your office goes on a little too long."

"That's because you don't like description. I'd still like to have some description of your house in there."

"I mean, does anyone really care that you have two neon lights hanging from the ceiling or that you lack toilet facilities?"

"I care. I like to know about the places where people live or work. I think it's important."

"It's important to you to know where the wall calendar is from?"

She stopped biting her nails. "If you're trying to start a fight—"

He looked bewildered. "A fight? I'm not trying to start a fight. Aren't we allowed to offer each other a little criticism?"

She knew she was being unfair. She knew if he were sitting there not surrounded by food her attitude would be a lot better. It was just so hard being in the same room with a man who never stopped snacking and never gained a pound.

"Okay," she said. "You're right, we should be able to critique each other's work."

"You sure?"

She nodded. "I'm sure."

"Well, moving on . . . This part likening me to Jeff Bridges. I feel that that's in retaliation for my saying you looked like Sissy Spacek."

"I said a younger, thinner Jeff Bridges."

"I don't look anything like Jeff Bridges."

"The point is, if I say you resemble Jeff Bridges, the readers have instant identification. Everyone goes to the movies. Anyway, it's not so much that you look like him, as you're the same type."

"I liked the ball player analogy."

"I thought you would."

"The part with the reporters was good."

"Thank you. Actually, I made them sound better than they were. Some of them were downright rude."

"You don't say much about Bobby."

"I didn't feel like it."

"I think you need some background on the two of you."

"I know, and I'll put it in eventually, but when I was writing it I was feeling very good about you and didn't want to spoil that feeling with a lot of talk about Bobby."

"Wait a minute. Do I get from that that at the moment you're not feeling so good about me?"

"That's not what I said."

"That's the feeling I'm getting."

"I don't want to talk about it."

He put down his notes and held out his arms. When she didn't immediately rush across the room into them, his expression became more serious. "If something's the matter, I think we should talk about it. Wasn't that one of the problems you had with Bobby, that you two didn't talk about your feelings?"

"It'll sound so petty."

"Yes, but it's the little, petty things that can screw up a relationship."

She avoided his eyes as she said, "Partly it's that candy bar sticking out of your pocket."

"I see. I was wondering when I read that part about the M&M candies. At first I thought you were exaggerating, trying to be funny, but then I wasn't so sure."

"Believe me, I wasn't trying to be funny. There's nothing funny about giving in to those kinds of impulses."

"It really bothers you when I eat candy around you?"

"Sometimes I could kill you."

"I guess we have a problem."

She sighed. "That's not really fair, though. It's my problem, not yours."

"I sure don't want to do anything that causes you to want to kill me half the time."

"It's not fair to make you go outside and eat your junk food, though."

"You're right, it isn't. Maybe you could go outside when I eat it."

She thought that was so unfair that she got up and started for the front door. Halfway there he caught up with her and took her in his arms. "Hey, I was only kidding."

"You should never have married me. This isn't going to work out."

"What're you talking about? I thought it was working out perfectly."

"You're always eating. Every time I look at you you're shoving something in your mouth. And when you're not eating, you have that pipe in your mouth."

"You object to my pipe?"

"No. I prefer it to the food. It's just that you have the same oral fixation I have, only I don't dare give in to mine."

"You chew your nails all the time."

She hid her hands behind her back. "I didn't think you'd noticed."

"I notice everything about you." He leaned down and kissed her, and then said, "Is this part of my oral fixation, wanting to kiss you all the time?"

"I guess it must be, because I feel the same way."

He took her by the hand and led her to the couch, and when they were settled with her in his arms, he said, "Just answer me one more question. Where was the instant attraction?"

"What instant attraction?"

"You said that in these books the hero and heroine were always instantly attracted to each other."

"If I hadn't been attracted, I wouldn't have gone out with you that night."

"You didn't go into it, though."

"Well, I'll tell you. In some books the heroine spends all her time thinking about the hero, but I just didn't have time that day. I had other things to do. I was attracted enough to go out with you, but I really barely knew you. It wasn't love at first sight or anything."

"I see."

"Was it with you? Is that why you asked me out right away?"

"I guess you'll find that out when you read my next chapter."

Chapter Four

Tom's first impression of Bobby had been this: he was the kind of guy who made obnoxious remarks to women in bars. He would also be the type to heckle stand-up comedians. Tom secretly admired that type of guy, while always professing to find them as obnoxious as did the woman he was with.

Tom had spent enough time in numerous bars and comedy clubs to have a handle on the type. Bobby was the kind of guy who would ease in next to a strange woman at the bar, flash her a boyish grin, and say, "Hey, baby, you ready for it?" And, while your average modern woman would either ignore him or tell him where to get off, there were still a few throwbacks to earlier times who actually *were* ready for it and didn't mind being asked. Bobby was the kind of guy who would be walking out of the bar with a woman he picked up before Tom had even smiled at his first woman. Bobby was the type even nice liberated women liked because he was up-front and cute with his chauvinism. Tom was the type of guy women had to really get to know well before they liked him.

As for being the type of guy who heckled stand-up comics, Tom, in the days when he was getting some experience at comedy clubs, always hoped for a few of them in any given audience. This was because Tom was better at handling hecklers than he was at writing comedy material and if he got enough hecklers, the audience generally loved him. If he didn't get hecklers, the audience generally ignored him. He rarely got booed and he concluded that they didn't care enough about him either way.

Tom was surprised when he found he was more successful in front of a jury than he ever had been in front of an audience. His sense of humor and timing were just good enough to lighten up things in the courtroom and keep the jury reasonably alert, but not good enough to satisfy hard-core comedy buffs. Judges were another thing altogether. In Tom's experience, judges rarely had senses of humor. That usually worked in Tom's favor as the judges almost never knew just why the jury was smiling and so were unable to call Tom on anything specific.

Bobby was also the kind of guy other men liked. He was the kind of guy who always knew the standings of the teams and the scores of the ball games, and while Tom also knew those things, he didn't know them with the same authority. Bobby, even if he got the score wrong, would be seen as such an expert that no one would argue with him. He was the kind of guy who'd always be willing to buy his buddies a drink or fix them up with women or give their car batteries a charge when it was needed. Bobby was a man's man. Tom, conversely, was a nut on sports, but he preferred the company of women.

Bobby also had the kind of looks women seemed to prefer. He had the dark curly hair that fell casually over his forehead and always made the nearest woman eager to push it back for him. He was exactly the height and build of men who strut: not too tall, muscular, big in the shoulders. And when they strutted into a place, women watched. Women never seemed to watch tall, thin men, the kind who often proved to be somewhat awkward. And Bobby had that real New York street accent, the kind that made him sound a little tough, a little dangerous and always sexy to women.

Tom's initial interview with Bobby in the jail had gone well.

"You my lawyer?" Bobby had asked him.

"That's up to you."

"My ex send you?"

Tom nodded.

"You a big criminal lawyer or something?"

"You're my first big criminal," said Tom.

That got a laugh from Bobby, and also a pleased look. The guy was actually flattered to be called a big criminal.

"You gonna get me off?"

"No, I'm going to get you sent up for life and run away with your ex."

That got an even bigger laugh from Bobby. "Hey, you're a pretty funny guy."

"My secretary tells me you're an Elvis impersonator."

"Yeah? She a fan of mine?"

"So it would seem."

"You an Elvis fan?"

"Well..."

"You're not. Elvis fans are all nuts. Fanatics. But man, when you're out on that stage and you really *feel* like Elvis, you start to see what all the craziness is about. I mean, that guy *had* it!''

Tom wondered if he would have been more successful if he had impersonated a dead comedian. He tried to think of a dead comedian but all he could come up with was Lenny Bruce, and he was too far from Tom's style. He could think of a few live ones he could impersonate, but unless they were dead it was considered stealing someone else's material.

Tom said, ''I think the DA's office will probably be willing to make a deal.''

''Down to what? Assault with a deadly weapon?''

''I don't know yet. I'll be talking to them later.''

Bobby shook his head. ''I done a lot of stupid things in my life, but that was the stupidest.''

''I guess you had your reasons.''

''You met my ex. You think she was worth it?''

''Worth getting life for?'' asked Tom. ''No, I don't think so.''

''I wasn't counting on anyone calling the cops. I thought it would be a little more private.''

''Well, you can always look at it this way—you've given Queens its own terrorist.''

Bobby almost fell out of his chair laughing at that one. Tom decided all he'd need would be a dozen Bobbys in any given audience and he'd have it made.

AT THE ARRAIGNMENT, Melinda Sussman, from the DA's office, asked for bail of fifty thousand. When Bobby winked at her and said softly, ''Oh, come on, baby,'' Melinda, who was a little too together to be Bobby's type, upped the ante to one hundred thousand. The judge knocked it back down to fifty when Tom pointed out that Bobby had no prior record, even though his client wasn't helping him any by not show-ing even a trace of remorse.

Before leaving his client, Tom again mentioned the possibility of plea bargaining, and Bobby was up for it. "Yeah, anything you could do along those lines would be great," Bobby told him.

When Tom walked out of the courthouse, he was surrounded by reporters who wanted to know if he was defending Bobby. It was the first time Tom had ever been surrounded by reporters, and it was a heady ex-perience. He felt just like Rudolph Giuliani, who was always giving press conferences that appeared on the nightly news. After saying he was defending Bobby, though, there wasn't much more he could say. He thought of telling them a few jokes, but decided not to press his luck.

It was an entirely different story from Bobby on plea bargaining when he appeared at Tom's office a cou-ple of hours later.

Jolene personally showed him in to see Tom, ob-viously thrilled to have a celebrity in their office.

"About the plea bargaining," said Bobby, looking around with interest at the neon signs.

"Would you like some coffee?" Jolene asked him, hovering in the doorway.

"You can bring us both coffee," said Tom.

When the coffee was brought in and Jolene had shut the door behind her, Tom asked, "What about the plea bargaining?"

"No can do," said Bobby.

"That wasn't the impression I got from the DA's office."

Bobby grinned. "I mean me. I'm not interested. I want to go for a trial."

Tom wanted a trial, too, but only for selfish reasons. He didn't think it would be in Bobby's best interests to go to court on this.

"What changed your mind?" Tom asked him.

"Well, my agent, for one thing. He's the one who bailed me out. It seems I made all the papers and the TV shows and, as a result, he's booked me a lot of club dates. He thinks there's even a chance I could get a shot at the Letterman show. I mean, the Letterman show? I'd have it made in the shade."

"None of which will do you a bit of good if you're up the river for twenty to life."

Bobby acknowledged this wisdom with a sheepish look. "I figure you can get me off. If we plea bargain, I'm going to have to do some time, aren't I?"

"Probably."

"So get me off. Flannery, my agent, figures you can plead temporary insanity."

Even agents knew the law these days. "They'll be expecting temporary insanity. You had to have been temporarily insane to hold a Weight Watchers meeting hostage."

"You saying you think I was nuts?"

"What I'm saying, Bobby, is that you must have been a little nuts at the time. Had you been drinking?"

"Nah, I was dead sober. I had it all planned out."

"If it was planned, I don't think we could plead temporary insanity."

"What other kinds of insanity are there?"

Tom opened his top drawer and took out a box of Jujubes. He passed it over to Bobby, who popped a few in his mouth. "I haven't had these for years," said Bobby. "Used to always eat them at the movies."

"They're good at the office, too." Tom tilted the box so that a dozen or so spilled into his mouth, then had to move them to the back of his mouth before his front teeth were glued shut and he couldn't talk.

"Tell me, Bobby, did you hear the voice of Elvis telling you to do it?"

Bobby looked incredulous. "Come on, man, you calling me seriously insane? You gonna ask me next if my *dog* told me to do it?"

"Why *did* you do it?"

"For love. Isn't that a good reason? I took a chance that if I did something that bizarre, maybe I could get Holly back."

"At a Weight Watchers meeting?"

Bobby shrugged. "It seemed fitting. If it weren't for Weight Watchers, we'd still be married."

"How long have you been divorced?"

"Two years."

"And you waited two years to try to get her back?"

"I figured she'd come back on her own, in her own time, but when I finally realized that wasn't gonna happen, I decided to speed things along."

Tom couldn't quite see a jury buying the defense of true love, but one never knew.

Bobby asked, "She'll probably testify against me, right?"

"I wouldn't be surprised."

"Talk to her, will you? Get her to drop the charges."

"It isn't up to her. Plus you held a lot of people hostage, and I don't think they'd all refuse to testify."

Bobby stood up. "Look, we can talk later, right? I got to show up for work, see if I still got a job."

It was after Bobby left that Tom got a sudden urge to ask Holly out to dinner. If someone had questioned him about why he was asking her out, he wouldn't have been able to adequately explain it. He thought it might have something to do with the fact that he wondered what it was about her that would make a man hold an entire room hostage in an effort to win her back. It only marginally had to do with the fact that she reminded him of Sissy Spacek.

It wasn't a smart move for a number of reasons. One was that he was pretty sure she'd turn him down. Another was it didn't seem kosher to be asking his client's ex-wife out on a date. Additionally, what would they talk about when they were constrained from discussing the case?

Despite all that, he still felt like asking her out.

He got out the telephone book and looked up Benson. There were a few dozen Bensons, but luckily she was listed under her full name. He punched out the number listed and was disappointed when he heard an answering machine picking up.

"Benson Bail Bond," the voice said. "No one's here right now, but if you leave a message I'll return your call as soon as possible."

When the beep came, Tom debated leaving a message versus hanging up. He finally left his name. If he changed his mind about asking her out, he could always just thank her for throwing business his way and leave it at that.

Bail bond? She was a bail bondsman? He had never run into a woman in the bail bond business. Usually it was a rather tough breed of men. That lent a little bit of intrigue to a possible date with her.

Which is why, when Holly called him back, he invited her out to dinner.

TOM HAD BEEN in trailers before, but never one like Holly's.

His first thought, when she opened the door and invited him in, was that he was stepping into an Amazon rain forest. He had never actually been in an Amazon rain forest, but he had seen them on National Geographic specials and knew what they looked like.

The forty-foot trailer was almost devoid of furniture, but what was there was made of bamboo. The walls and ceiling were painted pale green and there was green outdoor carpeting on the floor. Everywhere else—hanging from the ceiling, affixed to the walls, standing on the floor—there were plants, mostly of the fern variety, lit by unseen lighting. It was dense and green and hot and humid and he was sure if he listened closely he would hear the sound of jungle life.

Holly, in tight pink jodhpurs and a pink sweater, smiled up at him. "It doesn't feel like Queens, does it?" she asked.

It didn't even feel like the United States. "If I had as many neon lights as you have plants, I'd go blind."

"I guess you don't like it," she said, but she didn't sound in the least distressed by the fact.

Tom, who had already felt things crawling on him and who could hardly control a desire to scratch himself, didn't really know whether he liked it or not. It was interesting. It was different. He didn't think it was the kind of place where he could comfortably spend a night, however. Not that he in any way anticipated doing that.

He finally said, "Usually I figure I can tell something about a person by the way they live, but you've got me confused. Since you don't look like an Amazonian Indian..."

"Well, I'll tell you. It's a combination of appreciating the outdoors but preferring a controlled environment. This way I feel like an outdoorsy sort of person without having to contend with insects. I feel like I'm camping out but I have indoor facilities. Maybe I'm just weird."

Maybe she was. That was all right, he liked a little weirdness in people. People who didn't have a touch of weirdness to them were usually bland and uninteresting.

He waited while she put on a pink parka and mittens, then waited again while she locked all eleven locks on her door. As he led her to his car, he asked, "Who do all the cars belong to?"

"Me."

"You collect cars?"

"I take them as collateral. When I get enough, I'll quit the bail bond business and go into the used-car business."

He started the car and got the heater running. "You name it and we'll go there, but I seem to have an uncontrollable urge for pizza." Probably having to do with the fact that he'd never gotten any the night before. Maybe he would forever remember her as being partially responsible for Sal's not serving pizza the night before.

"No pizza," she said. She stated it as a matter of fact, not even being open to persuasion about it.

So okay. So she was the kind of woman who expected to be wined and dined on a date. He didn't mind putting out the money, it was just that his heart was set on pizza.

"How about Italian?"

"Pasta?"

"Yeah, Italian's usually pasta."

"I'd rather not," she said.

"You want to try a steak house?" He could get into a steak.

"How about a compromise? Are there any places where you could get a steak and I could get fish?"

"Fish? You like fish?"

"Don't you eat fish?"

"Not if I can help it," Tom answered her.

"You should. Do you have any idea what steak and pizza are doing to your cholesterol level?"

Tom didn't know, didn't care, and was afraid he was going to hear anyway. He ignored the question as being academic and instead reached over, opened the glove compartment, and grabbed the first thing that fell out. It turned out to be a Mounds bar.

"I keep a few candy bars in there in case I get hungry."

"It looks more like an arsenal in case of attack."

He figured she was trying to be funny and chuckled. "Want to share?" he asked her, already having torn the paper off and stuck half in his mouth.

"No, thank you."

He already had the feeling she was going to be a royal pain. He ought to go by the drive-through window at McDonald's, eat in the parking lot, then take her home. He was beginning to wonder what Bobby saw in her.

He found the kind of restaurant he usually avoided. The type that had a menu with every food known to man on it, specializing in nothing and nothing tasting very good. He didn't ask her permission before parking the car.

Once inside, she studied the menu as though she were memorizing it for a final exam. When the waiter hovered over the table, she finally looked up.

After a rather substantial silence, Tom said, "I'll have a New York cut, medium rare, french fries, and onion rings. Miller Lite, if you have it."

She was giving him the kind of look that made him feel like a member of a subspecies.

"Were you ordering for both of us?" she asked.

"Of course not," said Tom. He knew the rules. He knew women did their own ordering in restaurants.

"Is the sole broiled?" she asked the waiter.

"I think it's fried."

"Do you have any broiled fish?"

"I guess they could broil it for you," said the waiter.

"No butter on it," said Holly. "And have the chef weigh it. I don't want more than four ounces."

"Yes, ma'am. Any potatoes? We have baked, fried or mashed."

"No potatoes."

"Salad?"

"Yes. No dressing. And tea with lemon, please."

Tom was starving to death just hearing her order. Four ounces? He'd feed a cat more than four ounces.

"Is that going to be enough for you?" he asked her.

"It's enough for anyone," said Holly.

When the waiter brought the basket of rolls, Tom dug in, helping himself to a warm pumpernickel roll with raisins. He couldn't help noticing that her eyes were fixed on the roll. They watched as he broke it apart, spread a thick slab of butter on it, then raised it to his mouth. Only when it entered his mouth did her eyes shift away.

"Have one, they're great," said Tom, as soon as his mouth was no longer stuffed.

"No, thanks."

"Listen, this date was for dinner, wasn't it? Did you forget and eat before I arrived?"

"Not everyone has the need to consume ten thousand calories per meal."

"Oh, no! It entirely slipped my mind, I swear. I'm really stupid and I apologize. You were at Weight Watchers last night. You're on a diet."

"I am not on a diet."

"What are you, anorexic?"

"I've learned to eat correctly, that's all. I only eat when I'm hungry and I only eat what my body needs."

"Well, I happen to be hungry and my body needs a steak. And all the rest of it."

"I doubt it needs all that grease."

"You look all right to me, Holly, but if you think you're fat, that's okay, too. But I've always been on the skinny side and what I eat doesn't seem to affect that."

For a moment, the look in her eyes was of pure hatred. Then she made an effort at smiling. "No, I don't think I'm fat. But I once was, and I'm never going to be that way again."

Probably like his mother, who every time she gained five pounds thought she looked pregnant.

He decided that the best thing to do was get them off the subject of food. It was bad enough the food was going to be arriving any minute; they didn't have to talk about it, too.

"So," he said, searching for a conversational gambit, "how did you get in the bail bond business?"

"It was my dad's business. When he died, I took it over. What about you? How'd you get in the lawyer business?"

"It wasn't my ambition. What I wanted to be was a stand-up comic."

"You?"

"Yeah, I know what you're thinking, that I ought to be funny. Well, that's what the audience thought, too, which got to be something of a problem."

She looked more animated than she had been all night. "I can't imagine you as a stand-up comic."

"A lot of people couldn't. My family, my friends, the managers of the comedy clubs..."

She was starting to smile. "Go on, do some more."

"That wasn't part of a routine."

"It sounded like one. It was pretty funny."

"So tell me, is Bobby's Elvis act any good?"

Her smile faded. "We're not supposed to be discussing Bobby."

"He wasn't arrested for being a bad Elvis impersonator. It really has nothing to do with the case."

"You ought to catch his act sometime. He's at the Skylark—"

"Lounge. I know. My secretary's a fan of his."

"She looked more intelligent than that."

"My thought exactly."

"Yeah, he's good. But so are hundreds of others. He dragged me to an Elvis impersonator convention once and there were Elvises crawling out of the woodwork."

"That'd make a pretty funny comedy routine."

"Remind me to tell you about it sometime."

"Thanks, but I don't do it any longer. Now I'm a serious lawyer, soon to be a major criminal lawyer."

"If Bobby's your major criminal, lots of luck."

"He wants to plead—" He broke off just in time. "Sorry, I can't talk about that."

"Well, it's got to be insanity, because what he pulled last night was insane."

"Really, we can't talk about this."

She was looking past him. "Well, we're not going to have to because I think the long procession of waiters arriving are bearing your food."

The food wasn't particularly good, but it was filling, and that was what was important.

He noticed that she ate very slowly so that they finished at about the same time. He had seen a chocolate cake revolving in a glass case when they had arrived, and he called the waiter over.

"Would you care for some dessert?" asked the waiter.

He looked at Holly, who shook her head. "I'll have a piece of that chocolate cake," he said, "with a scoop of ice cream on top. And another Miller."

"Coffee for the lady?" asked the waiter.

"I'm fine," said Holly.

"It's really none of my business," said Tom, "but you don't seem in a very good mood tonight."

"Believe me, it's better than last night."

"I should've realized. You probably would've liked to stay home and rest after that experience. I've read that being a hostage can be traumatizing."

"Bobby even without a gun can be traumatizing. Sorry, I didn't mean to bring him up."

"It's not your fault, I brought up the subject."

"Anyway, I'm not traumatized. A little angry, maybe. One of my customer's jumped bail today."

"Does that happen often?"

"Not very. But I'm going to have to find him."

"You're going after some criminal on your own?"

Holly smiled. "He's essentially harmless. He's an artist who decided printing money was more lucrative. This time, though, he was going to do a few years and I think he panicked."

His dessert arrived and he saw her avert her eyes from the table. It was pretty humiliating to be out on a dinner date with a woman who was sickened by the sight of him eating. He had a better time eating alone.

When he was finished, he sneaked a look at his watch, saw that it wasn't even seven-thirty yet, and faked a yawn. "I don't know about you," he said, "but I'd just as soon make an early night of it. You probably didn't get much sleep last night either." If he hustled, he could make it home before the Knicks game started.

He thought she looked amused. "No, I didn't. I'd just as soon head on home."

He broke a few speed limits getting her back to her trailer, and when she said, "No, don't get out, I can walk myself to the door," he didn't demur.

She paused outside his car for a moment before closing the door. "Thank you for the dinner," she said in a very polite voice.

He tried to put some enthusiasm into his voice when he said, "My pleasure. We'll have to do it again sometime."

She merely smiled at that, not committing herself either way, then slammed his door shut.

He had never felt so relieved in his life.

Interlude

He knew by this time that her eating habits were a pretty good indicator of her moods. The fact that while she was reading his latest chapter she had felt the necessity to first go to the kitchen for a diet drink, then back almost immediately for an ounce of unbuttered popcorn, followed by a small apple, one of those tasteless dietetic candy bars plus some celery sticks, told him that something he had written had caused her stress.

He finally went to the kitchen himself, deciding to stay there until she had finished. Anyway, he was trying to do his eating in the kitchen these days. She stayed out of the room when at all possible, and this left him free to raid the refrigerator and cupboards out of range of her eagle eyes.

He was scarfing down a bowl of cold spaghetti he had found hidden in the back of the refrigerator when she appeared in the doorway. Something about her expression didn't bode well for his chapter, and by this time he knew it had nothing to do with grammar or syntax or style. It had to with content, and he had a feeling he was in trouble.

"I feel I have two choices," she said.

He said, "What I was thinking was, maybe we ought to take a drive to the mall and look at that patio furniture you were talking about."

"Good try."

"I guess we're not going to the mall."

"My first choice is to load up my plants and move back to my trailer."

"It was that bad?"

"And my second choice is to kill you."

"And your third choice is we go into the living room and discuss this like rational adults."

"I'm not feeling like a rational adult."

He nodded. He could see that. He was feeling a little stress himself, so he reached up into the cupboard where he kept his stash of candy bars, but as he did so, he got this creepy feeling. Like as he was reaching for the candy, she was coming up behind him with a butcher knife in her hand.

He stopped reaching and turned around. No butcher knife, but if eyes could kill . . .

"Can we for once have a conversation during which you don't continuously eat?"

"Can I smoke my pipe?"

"You know I have no objection to your pipe."

His only objection to his pipe was the fact that it was forever going out.

She turned to go into the living room and he followed her. She took a seat in one of the chairs, which didn't seem friendly, and he went over to the couch. He picked up his pipe from the coffee table, shoved the bowl of caramel corn out of reach, and began to fill his pipe. He took his time. He told himself that until the pipe was going, nothing was going to be said.

He was wrong. She started in anyway. "The first thing I'd like to say," she said, "is that this book was supposed to be a romance."

"I know what you're going to say, that there was nothing romantic about that chapter."

"There was nothing romantic about that chapter."

"That was your fault, though."

She gave him a tight smile that was less like a smile than no smile at all.

He puffed on his pipe for a few moments. "It's just that your chapter, the one before, wasn't romantic, either. When you weren't instantly attracted to me, then I figured we were going for authenticity, and you know as well as I do that our first date was a disaster."

"I hadn't known it was *that* bad. I mean, the chapter ends with you taking me home and thinking to yourself that you've never been so relieved in your life!"

"Come on, be honest. I bet you didn't go into your trailer and cry your eyes out over it."

"Yes, but I didn't have anything against you personally. I just vowed never to eat with you again."

"And instead you married me and we'll be eating together the rest of our lives." At least he hoped they would.

"It's a problem."

"Our marriage."

"The eating part."

"I see." His pipe went out and he slowly got it relit. "How much of a problem?"

"Pretty serious. It's not like you only eat at meals. Except when you're sleeping, you eat pretty continuously."

"I don't eat when we're making love."

She smiled.

"Or when I'm taking a shower."

"Maybe we should just talk about the chapter. I don't think a reader, who is expecting a romance, is going to find that chapter very satisfying. The hero meets the heroine, they go out on a date, and they don't like each other?"

"But this is different," he said. "Maybe they don't like each other in that chapter, but eventually they do."

"In some books they've made love by this point."

He wasn't sure he had heard her right. "They made love on the first date?"

"Well, once in a while, but if that happens it's usually a case of love at first sight. It's just that we've spent a lot of time on other things and haven't concentrated on the love story."

"Without the other things, all we'd *have* is a love story. Isn't there supposed to be anything else?"

"Very often they're caught up in some adventure or another. Usually there's a conflict between them."

"All right," he said, "there you are. Food was our conflict."

"It still is, but I'm not sure that's the kind of conflict we should have."

"Well, if you want, I can go back and revise and have us making mad, passionate love in that jungle of yours."

"It wouldn't be believable."

"It would if you had been different at dinner."

"You mean if I had stuffed myself like a pig?"

"Look, what if it had been different? What if you had said yes to pizza? If you had done that, I probably would have invited you back to my place to watch the Knicks game.''

"I wish you had. As it was, I went home and watched the game by myself.''

"I wish I'd known that.''

"But even if you had invited me back with you, we wouldn't have ended up making love.''

"You can't know that for sure. What if the Knicks had won, and carried away by the excitement of the moment, you had thrown yourself into my arms and it had just naturally progressed from there?''

She chuckled. "I don't get carried away that easily.''

"Oh, I don't know about that. Why don't you come over here and sit beside me?''

"Well, I wouldn't have gotten carried away that easily on a first date. I was pretty wary of men at that time. Anyway, I think it's probably better that we don't have a love scene that early on. Then we'd have to manufacture something to keep us apart so that later, when we got back together, it would be satisfying.''

"Are we constrained to follow some kind of pattern here?''

"Well, it usually goes like this—they meet, they fall in love, something keeps them apart, and in the end they get back together.''

"Can't that be tampered with?''

"Sometimes it is, but I'm always surprised.''

"I say the hell with it. Let's go with what really happened, and if they don't like it, too bad. I happen to think it's a pretty good story.''

"I think I'm beginning to realize why they end when the hero and heroine get married.''

"That's a natural ending."

"Yes, but that way you also don't have to show all the problems that come up later. Problems that aren't so romantic."

"Like my eating habits."

She nodded.

"Is it getting to be a very bad problem for you?"

"Don't get mad at me, but I think you need help."

"*Help?* I hope you're not suggesting what I think you're suggesting."

"I knew you'd get mad."

"What do you want me to do, join Fat Busters? I'm not overweight!"

"Nevertheless, you have an eating disorder."

"Only in your mind. I think I have a pretty healthy appetite."

"Maybe you should see—"

"If you say shrink—"

"I was thinking of someone who specializes in behavior modification."

"Damn it, I don't want to modify my behavior. I'm happy and well adjusted just the way I am."

"All right, but would you do one thing for me?"

He said, "I'm not making any promises until I hear it."

"Would you go to a doctor and get your blood pressure and cholesterol checked? You could be killing yourself and not even know it."

"I can't believe I'm hearing this."

"You should get a physical once a year anyway."

"But I'm in perfect health!"

"That's what they always say about men who suddenly drop dead of heart attacks."

"You trying to scare me?"

"I guess so. Just a little. But do it for me, okay? So I won't worry about you?"

"All right, but only to prove you're wrong. And only if you'll come over here and sit next to me and stop giving me such a hard time."

She hesitated only a moment, then went across the room and sat beside him. His arm naturally found its way around her shoulders.

"Isn't that better?" he asked her.

"It makes me nervous being within eating distance of a bowl of caramel corn."

"Forget the caramel corn—you're within kissing distance of me."

"You know, if I had known how relieved you were to get rid of me that night, I never would have called you and asked you out. Which means that we wouldn't be sitting here today married."

"Aren't you glad you did?"

"You don't understand. The only reason we're married is because I didn't have all the facts."

"Look, if I had been all that relieved to get rid of you, I wouldn't have said yes when you called me."

"Why did you say yes?"

"You're going to have to wait to find out."

"I don't know. I'm beginning to think that maybe writing this book is dangerous. We're finding out all these things that maybe we should've known before we got married."

"But doesn't that make it more interesting?"

"I'm not sure."

He tilted her chin so that their faces were close, and then he kissed her. Her lips were warm and responsive and he thought he should have done this much earlier and avoided all the arguing altogether.

When he finally came up for air, he asked, "Do you want to continue the critique or do you want to adjourn to the bedroom?"

"I guess we can always continue the critiquing afterward."

"Just so long as it's my chapter you're critiquing and not my lovemaking."

"Speaking of which . . ."

He let out a moan. "Oh, no, don't tell me you have a problem with that, too."

"Only a slight one. Why do we always have to go to the bedroom?"

He slid down on the couch and pulled her on top of him. "No reason at all," he told her. "Absolutely no reason at all."

Chapter Five

John Sykol's record showed that the owner of a local art gallery had made his bail. While Holly didn't remember the owner other than the fact that he was male, she was pretty sure she would be remembered, as women bail bondspersons weren't commonplace. Not having anything else to go on, she decided to drop by the gallery.

She had never seen John's work. Well, that wasn't quite true, she had seen the twenty-dollar bills he had designed and printed. They had been extremely good work except that the feel of the paper had been wrong. Which meant that John had been caught almost immediately when trying to deposit a large amount of them into his bank account.

The gallery was in a house in a neighborhood now zoned commercial. It was an ugly house made uglier by the coat of pink paint with the lavender trim. A sign over the door said Cooperative des Artistes.

The door to the gallery was locked but a sign posting the hours said it should be open, so she rang the doorbell. She was expecting the man who had made bail for Sykol, but it was a woman who came to the door. She was wearing paint-splattered jeans and a flannel shirt and some of the paint had gotten into her short, punk haircut.

"You looking for someone?" asked the woman.

"I just wanted to look around at the art," said Holly, trying to sound like an art patron.

The woman became more friendly. "Oh, sure, come on in." She held the door open for Holly, and Holly knocked the snow off her boots before entering.

She knew Sykol's exhibit without being told. They were enormous collages in which twenty-dollar bills figured prominently. Pasted onto or beneath or beside the newly printed money, were headlines from the *Wall Street Journal* and other newspapers all having to do with the collapse of the stock market or the worsening economy. They weren't the kind of thing Holly would want hanging over her couch, or even her bed, but they were striking. She wouldn't mind having one in her office, although some of her customers might try peeling off the fake currency.

"That's John Sykol's work," said the woman, obviously disappointed that Holly hadn't paused to look at the florals she had been pointing out to her.

"They're very interesting," said Holly. "He makes a very bold statement."

"That's his latest style. He used to do paintings of children hanging out of the windows of welfare hotels, but no one bought them."

"Are people buying these?"

"I think they would if enough people saw them. You're the first customer we've had this week. I'm beginning to think people in Rocky Inlet aren't interested in art."

"What's the price on this one?" asked Holly, pointing to the largest. There were no prices affixed to the canvasses.

"John said to ask a thousand, but he'd probably go down in price."

"I really like it," said Holly, wondering if she looked like the kind of person who could afford a thousand-dollar canvas.

"I guess you could talk to John about it."

"Is he here?"

"Not at the moment, but he calls in every couple of days to see if anything has sold. John's a real optimist."

"Could you give me his number? I'd like to talk to him about buying it."

The woman shook her head. "I don't know his number. But if you leave me your number, I could have him call you."

Holly gave her her home number. She'd simply change the tape on her machine so he wouldn't recognize the name of the bail bond business when he called. On the way out, Holly paused by the florals, saying, "These are really lovely," hoping to cheer her up. The woman brightened up for a minute, but when Holly didn't seem interested in buying, she sank back into dejection. Feeling guilty for having induced the dejection, Holly said, "I may be back for one of those, too."

And she might. It would be the perfect Christmas gift for her mother, whose taste was all in her mouth.

"I have a Christmas special on them," the woman said. "They're only thirty dollars."

Holly took pity on her. She might be suffering a financial reversal at the moment, but the bail bond business had to be better than selling bad paintings out of a gallery no one went to. Plus, thirty dollars was a small price to pay to get in touch with Sykol.

Holly picked one out wherein the flowers matched her mother's throw cushions, paid for it in cash and made the woman's day.

Thus reminded of her mother, Holly decided to stop by and see her before heading back to work. She'd had numerous phone messages from her, none of which she had returned. She was still miffed at her mom's appearance on TV, but it shouldn't have surprised her. Marilyn Benson was the garrulous sort whose main ambition in life was to get on one of the numerous game shows she was addicted to.

Holly rang the bell of the house, then let herself in with a key. Her mom preferred it that way. Anything that would prevent Marilyn from having to get up out of her chair and walk to the door was encouraged.

"It's me, Mom," yelled Holly, heading back to the living room.

The room was overheated, the TV was on, and Marilyn, wearing a flowered housecoat was ensconced in her late husband's made-to-order Lazy Boy recliner.

"There's Danish in the kitchen," were the first words out of Marilyn's mouth.

"Hi, Mom."

"You can heat them up in the microwave while you're at it and bring the whole plate in."

Holly had learned to tune out any talk of food from her mother. She took a seat in the chair next to the TV so that her mother had to see her while she watched the show. "Everyone okay?" she asked her.

Her mother waited for a commercial and then turned her gaze to Holly. "You look sick. You been to a doctor?"

"I've never felt better," said Holly.

Her mother gave her a sly look. "Well, I guess that Weight Watchers place finally paid off for you."

"Right, Mom. I joined so that someday I could appear on the eleven o'clock news."

"Poor Bobby. I hope you bailed him out."

"Poor *Bobby*! Mom, the guy was crazy. He held an entire meeting at gunpoint."

"You know Bobby. He's used to being onstage. He was just using that gun like he uses a microphone."

"Am I hearing you right? You think there's nothing wrong with what Bobby did?"

"Your sister thinks it's romantic."

"And you, Mom? Do you think it's romantic?"

"You're tearing the boy apart, Holly. You've taken away his reason for living."

"Right. He doesn't have anyone to abuse anymore."

"He never lifted a hand to you!"

"No, but his mouth never stopped."

"I want you to come over to supper Saturday night, Holly. Your brother and sister have been asking about you, and the whole family hasn't been together since Thanksgiving."

"This isn't going to be a little surprise, is it? You're not inviting some reporters by to eat?"

Marilyn had the grace to look embarrassed. "I know I got a little carried away, but those reporters just wouldn't leave me alone. Practically camped on my doorstep. Did you see the picture of me in *Newsday*?"

"I must've missed that one."

"I haven't heard from a one of them today, so I doubt they'll be by Saturday night. What I was thinking, though, is that I should ask Bobby over. You two could get a chance to talk it out."

"Mom, there's nothing to talk out."

"Bobby always was a pleasure at the dinner table what with all those Elvis stories of his."

"Mom, I have no intention of seeing Bobby again until I see him in court."

"Surely you're not suing him over this."

"You can't do what Bobby did and not get arrested."

"Do it for *me*, Holly. I haven't seen Bobby in an age."

Holly took a deep breath and lied. "I can't do that, Mom. I'm seeing someone."

Her mother picked up the remote control and the TV set went dead. "Would you repeat that?"

"I said I'm seeing someone."

"A man?"

"Of course a man."

"I wish you'd find a man for your sister." When Holly didn't reply to this, she said, "What's he do for a living?"

"He's an attorney."

There was the beginning of a smile on her mother's fat face. "A professional man."

"Yes."

"Well, bring him along to dinner. I'd like to meet him."

"He might be busy Saturday night, Mom."

"Busy? On date night? At least you can ask him and find out."

"I'll ask."

"What're you doing here, anyway? Why aren't you at work making us some money?"

Holly got up. "I'm on my way. I just thought I'd stop by and see how you're doing."

"We'll expect you Saturday. You and that lawyer."

IF SHE DIDN'T HAVE enough problems, now she had made an additional one for herself. She had two equally distasteful options: she could show up at her mother's alone Saturday night and have to listen to talk of Bobby all through dinner, or she could call a man she had never anticipated going out with again and invite him to a family dinner.

It was crazy. The crazy part was, Tom was bound to love her mother's cooking. He'd be so stuffed with all the wrong kinds of food that he'd think he was in heaven. The problem was, he'd also think she was interested in him. She'd had some unfortunate dates in her life, but none had been as unfortunate as that dinner with Tom.

He'd get the wrong idea, of course. He'd get the idea that she wanted to see him again. But it would be worth it if it got her mother off her back about Bobby, and it wasn't as though she'd have to see him again after Saturday night. If he called to reciprocate she'd just say no.

It took her most of the afternoon to get up her nerve to call him. She had never called a man and asked him out before. At least a dozen times she picked up the phone, dialed, and then hung up before the phone was answered at the other end. Her behavior was juvenile and unprofessional and she felt like a fool, but the nagging question in the back of her mind was, What if he says no? If she felt like a fool just for calling him, how would she feel then?

In the old days she would have consumed five candy bars just to calm her nerves. Now she tried to imagine the very worst that could happen so that she would be prepared for it. She imagined him hanging up on her, telling her the last thing he felt like doing Saturday night was going to dinner at her mother's, or pretending he didn't remember her. All would be embarrassing, but not something she couldn't live through. After all, being turned down for a date wasn't life threatening.

She began to feel what it must be like for a man to be constantly courting rejection.

When she finally summoned up her nerve to let the phone ring until his secretary picked up, it was almost anticlimactic when she was put through to him and he remembered very well who she was.

"Hi. What's happening?" he asked her.

"Not much," she said, while telling herself to just ask him and get it over with.

There was a silence and she could tell he was wondering why she had called. He finally said, "If you're worried, Bobby hasn't jumped bail yet."

"Bobby won't jump bail. He'll love all the publicity of a trial."

"That was my assessment."

There was another silence and she finally took a deep breath and plunged right in. "I was wondering if you'd want to have dinner at my mother's house Saturday night. You're probably busy, though."

"Saturday night?"

"Yes."

"Well . . ."

"You'll love her cooking. I'm sure she'll have something of everything, she usually does. You could gain twenty pounds just looking at my mother's dinners."

"That sounds pretty good," he said.

"Well, I just thought I'd ask."

"What time?"

"She eats early. Probably around six."

"Yea, I guess I could make that. Should I meet you there or pick you up or what?"

She figured he was thinking if he met her there he could escape early. Which was all right with her except he might get there early and be cross-examined by her mother. "Why don't I pick you up?"

"That'll be a change," he said, and gave her his address.

She still felt stupid after she had hung up. He hadn't exactly jumped at the chance to see her again. It sounded more like he didn't know how to gracefully turn her down, which was a problem she often had and could relate to.

Still, all in all, it was a whole lot better than having her mother invite Bobby.

WHEN SHE PICKED HIM UP on Saturday night she was surprised to see he lived in a house. She didn't know any single guys who had their own houses. Most of them either still lived at home or had an apartment. Bobby had immediately moved back home after the divorce, but then Bobby was incapable of taking care of himself. Bobby liked a live-in laundress and cook and housekeeper.

Tom had even put a wreath on the door and might have had a Christmas tree, but he didn't invite her in so she didn't find out.

"This is going to be great getting a home-cooked meal," he told her as they walked to her car. "My parents always eat out."

"Mother doesn't think the servings are large enough at restaurants."

"They usually aren't," he said.

Holly thought they were usually three times too much, but it seemed useless to argue over it when she didn't contemplate ever being in a restaurant again with him. He was being sweet about it, though. The invitation to dinner must have come as a complete surprise to him.

Holly wondered whether to prepare him for her family. She decided there was no way to prepare him for them; he'd have to see them in person to believe them.

Her mother's house was only a ten-minute drive from where he lived and Holly drove the icy streets carefully, in no hurry for the evening to begin.

"Is it just going to be your mother?" he asked her.

"No, my brother and sister will be there. Tiffany's three years younger than me and Pee Wee's still in college."

"Pee Wee? You actually call him that?"

"If we'd started calling him that he probably would've balked, but his teammates in high school gave him the nickname and so he loves it."

"Basketball?"

"No, football."

"This is going to be great having a family dinner."

She thought he was maybe even being nicer about it than he had to be. "Are you an only child?"

"No. My family's just not much on family dinners. They're not even going to be around at Christmas."

Holly couldn't imagine a family not around at Christmas. Or maybe she could, but only in her wildest dreams. Her family would never miss a holiday that involved food.

"I guess last night was kind of a bust," he said.

She thought of lying, saying it had been great, but she had had to do so much lying in her marriage that she never felt like having to do it again. "It was okay," she said, which was only stretching the truth a little.

"I think it's pretty open-minded of you to give it another shot. I was surprised when you called."

Well, she had asked for it by asking him out. Now he was going to think she was interested in him just because she had tried to appease her mother. Lying to anyone—this time her mother—never ended up doing any good. No, that wasn't exactly true. If it kept her from having her mother ask Bobby over, then anything was worth it. Her mother was just not going to let go of the fantasy of Holly and Bobby getting back together again. Her mother had the misguided notion that any husband was better than none.

"I find dating very tricky," said Holly.

"You noticed that? The thing is, you never know where you stand with a person. There's all this game playing going on. Take last night. I really get tired of eating alone, and I figured, you put me onto a case, why not take you out for a meal? But then, I don't know, you could've told me where you wanted to eat. I'm not that particular about where I eat."

"Don't worry about it. I'm paying you back for that overcooked fish by making you eat my mother's cooking."

"She's not a good cook?"

"I don't know whether she's good or not. I swear, though, if I didn't think you'd like it, I wouldn't have invited you."

"That's good enough for me," said Tom.

Holly parked in front of her mother's house. Should she warn him? Should she give him any clue? Or should she just let him walk into the fun house unawares?

She didn't have the guts to warn him.

Her sister Tiffany, weighing in at 285, answered the door. Her waist-length blond hair was hanging loose, her body was encased in a violet sweater dress that had to be hand knit because that size couldn't have been mass produced, and a multitude of jewelry clanked every time she moved.

"Hi, Tiff," said Holly. "I'd like you to meet Tom. This is my sister, Tiffany."

"This is really nice of you folks to have me over," said Tom, grasping Tiffany's hand and beaming at her.

So far he hadn't fainted. She'd move on to her brother. Pee Wee, weighing in at 314, was in the living room devouring a bowl of corn chips. He was in sweat pants and a T-shirt and his hair—the best in the family—had been shorn of most of its curls. "Hey, Pee Wee," said Holly, "this is Tom."

"What do you say?" said Pee Wee. "Can I get you a beer?"

"Love one," said Tom, making himself at home on the couch. One hand was already reaching for the corn chips.

Holly saw her mother, weighing in at 308, peering through the kitchen door. "Hey, Mom, come and meet Tom."

Marilyn, in a black polyester pantsuit and a fuchsia apron, moved gracefully into the living room. "Dinner will be ready in a minute, Tom," she told him. "I'm real glad you could join us."

"Smells great," said Tom.

Round one began with a salad and a plate of spaghetti. Holly ignored the spaghetti and paced herself on the salad. It was probable that it would be the only thing served she cared to eat.

Tom finished the spaghetti and had seconds. He and Pee Wee discussed the Knicks. Holly, who was also a Knicks fan, could have entered into the conversation, but she wasn't sure she wanted Tom to know they had anything in common.

Round two was the main course, consisting of pot roast, mashed potatoes and gravy, corn and biscuits. Holly kept her salad in front of her. There wasn't any dinner conversation to speak of because everyone else was too busy eating. Marilyn and Tiffany had seconds. Tom and Pee Wee had thirds and probably would have had fourths, but Marilyn reminded them to leave some room for dessert.

Round three was dessert, and her mom had outdone herself. There was chocolate pie with tons of whipped cream and each of them consumed a fourth of the pie. Holly made herself a cup of tea.

It hadn't been easy sitting and watching them eat. She didn't have a superior feeling knowing that she was eating for her health and they weren't, because her reason for losing weight had never had anything to do with health. She didn't feel superior knowing she was thin while the rest of her family was still fat, either, because for most of her life she had eaten and looked just like them, and right now she was only a thin line away from reaching out and grabbing some of that chocolate pie and shoving it into her mouth. She wondered if she'd ever get over the hunger.

When dinner was over, Pee Wee invited Tom down to the recreation room in the basement to shoot a game of pool, and Holly offered to help her mother and Tiffany clean up.

"You'll do no such thing," said her mother, carrying a load of plates out into the kitchen. "All you dirtied was one little bowl. Tom had a nice appetite, though."

"He seems very nice," said Tiffany.

"Don't think you fooled me, though," said her mother. "You two act as though you hardly know each other. I figured you invited him along so as I wouldn't invite Bobby."

"Oh, Mom, she doesn't want to see Bobby," said Tiffany.

"I thought he'd enjoy a home-cooked meal," said Holly.

"Well, that's all right, you bring him over anytime," said Marilyn, "but don't try to palm him off as your boyfriend because I know better."

"We only met recently," said Holly. "He took me out to dinner last night."

"Well, he seems very nice," said Tiffany. She cast a worried glance at her mother and said, "Mom, should I tell her?"

"Tell me what?" asked Holly.

"Holly's not going to care," said Marilyn.

"What are you talking about?" asked Holly.

Tiffany blushed a bright pink. "I'm going with some friends from work to see Bobby tonight. They were real impressed he was married to my sister."

Holly wasn't surprised to hear it. Tiffany had had a crush on Bobby since the first time he had been to their house, and it hadn't abated in the years Holly had been married to him. She sometimes thought Tiffany would have been the perfect wife for him. She was used to being her mother's slave at home, her boss's at the office, and probably would have taken Bobby's orders and thought she was in heaven. She probably would even tolerate the other women in his life.

"I don't care if you go to the Skylark," said Holly. "I just hope you weren't cheering him on the other night."

"I just couldn't believe Bobby would do something like that," said Tiffany. "I never knew he was so romantic."

"There was nothing romantic about being humiliated in front of an entire meeting," said Holly. "Nor did the police find anything romantic about Bobby having a gun."

"One of the girls at work wants your autograph," said Tiffany. "I told her you probably wouldn't—"

"You were right," said Holly.

"You know we had to make reservations for tonight? The Skylark's expecting their biggest crowd in history."

"I wouldn't put it past Bobby to have done it for the publicity," said Marilyn. "He always had a good head on him."

"I'd agree with you," said Holly, "if I hadn't been there myself. He was a little crazy that night. He was in one of those moods he always got in if he couldn't get his own way. What he needed was his mother there to yell at him."

"You don't need to stay in the kitchen with us, Holly," said her mother. "Why don't you take some beer and pretzels down to the boys?"

Tom looked almost ecstatic that he was being brought beer and pretzels, and he gave Holly a smile of such sweetness that she had a momentary twinge about getting him there under false pretenses.

She sat on a bar stool and watched them finish their game. Like her brother, she associated pool with beer and a snack, the way she associated going to the movies with buttered popcorn and a large Coke and chocolate-covered raisins, and the beach with hotdogs and hamburgers and fries. She hadn't enjoyed doing any of them in two years. Hell, even birthdays weren't the same without birthday cake and ice cream, and if she ever had to go to another catered wedding she might cut her throat.

When they finished the game, Pee Wee excused himself, saying he was meeting his friends, and Tom asked her if she wanted to play.

"Mom probably has the Knicks game on if you want to watch," she told him.

"You wouldn't mind?"

"Not at all. We're all Knicks fans."

"I'm really having a great time," Tom told her, following her up the stairs. "I like your family."

"Well, it's mutual—they like you."

Her mother already had the coffee table filled with enough snacks to last through the game. She also had a scrapbook she was starting with all the articles about the hostage situation and several photos of herself.

"I taped myself on the news, too," Marilyn told them. "If you want to see them, I'll put them on after the game."

"I'm sure we already saw them, Mom."

On top of the TV set was a wedding picture of Holly and Bobby which her mother refused to get rid of. Holly noticed Tom's eyes straying to it several times.

Finally, during a commercial, he asked her, "Is that you and Bobby?"

"I'm afraid so."

He got up and walked over to take a closer look at it. Instead of any of the remarks she had anticipated, though, he said, "You made a good-looking couple."

Holly could tell her mother was dying to jump in with some remark about the perfect couple but was managing to restrain herself. She did tell Tom, though, that she had made Holly's wedding dress.

"You're amazing," said Tom. "My mother can't cook *or* sew."

"What does she do?" asked Holly.

"She's a pediatrician."

"Oh, well, now, that's important work," said Marilyn. "Take me, though, I was always happy to stay home and be a housewife. You can have commuting to work every day of your life. My daughters, sorry to say, don't take after me though. Holly took over the family business and Tiffany always had her sights set on being an executive secretary."

Holly said, "Tom wanted to be a comedian."

"You tell jokes?" Marilyn asked him.

"Not jokes, exactly, more like routines."

"I just love Rodney Dangerfield," said Marilyn. "You as funny as him?"

"If I was as funny as him," said Tom, "I wouldn't be a lawyer."

"Go on," said Marilyn, "make me laugh."

Holly started to giggle at Tom's look of consternation.

"I'm a little out of practice," said Tom.

"We don't care," said Marilyn. "It's always nice to have a good laugh after you eat. Keeps you healthy."

Tom looked at Holly and shrugged, then moved to the middle of the floor. With an expectant look, Marilyn turned down the sound on the TV.

Tom smiled, as though at an audience. "Have you noticed how no one talks on the phone anymore? It used to be, I'd meet a woman and think I might want to take her out, so I'd call her up, want to talk a little, maybe get to know her a little on the phone, but I'd get her machine. So I'd leave a message on her machine, and the next thing I'd know I'd get a message from her on my machine. So I'd call back, but it would be her machine again, so I'd ask her if she'd want to go out on Saturday night. Well, she'd call back and get my machine and say okay, so by the time I'd actually see her on Saturday night I already felt intimate with her machine, but I didn't know her."

Marilyn said, "Isn't that the truth. You forgot about 'call waiting,' though. That's a real pain in the neck."

"You didn't laugh," said Tom, taking a seat on the couch.

"I smiled, though," said Marilyn. "Were we supposed to laugh?"

"I think it was the delivery," said Holly. "You didn't really seem into it. I imagine that's because you're in a strange living room with only two in the audience."

"They didn't laugh at the clubs, either," said Tom.

"Did you write your own material?" Holly asked him.

Tom nodded. "You think that was a mistake?"

"Listen, I couldn't have done it," said Holly. "I can't even remember a joke five seconds after I hear it."

"I got one for you," said Marilyn. "What weighs three thousand pounds and growls?"

"I don't know," said Tom. "What?"

"A Weight Watchers meeting."

Tom grinned and Holly shook her head.

"I made that up myself," said Marilyn. "I thought it was pretty good."

"Maybe you should write my material," said Tom.

After the basketball game, Marilyn talked them into a couple of games of gin rummy, and by the time they left it was after one.

"We could've left after dinner," Holly told him as she drove him home.

"What for? I had a great time."

"You were really nice about it."

"Listen, it was easy. Everyone made me feel right at home. And you were right, your mom's a great cook. I don't think I needed that pecan pie when we were playing cards, though."

"I'm glad I invited you."

"I am, too. You know something? You do better dates than I do."

"This wasn't a date. This was just a family dinner."

"Something tells me it would've been a shame if we'd left it at last night."

Something was telling Holly the same thing. He might have a real eating disorder, but he also had all the qualities she had found lacking in Bobby. He was a good, decent man, and he was also appealing, and that combination wasn't to be found all that often.

Holly pulled up in front of his house and parked. He started to thank her for the evening, but she interrupted him. "No, I want to thank you. Sometimes I get a little annoyed with my family, but you seemed to bring out the best in all of us. I really enjoyed having you along."

"You going to walk me to the door and kiss me good-night?" he asked her.

Holly chuckled. "I hadn't planned on it."

"You call me up, you ask me for a date, and then you refuse to walk me to the door and kiss me goodnight? If you're worried about a rejection, I already decided it was okay to kiss you on the second date."

"Oh, well, in that case," said Holly, opening up her door and getting out. She ran around the side of the car with the idea of opening his door for him, but she slipped on the ice and landed on her rear end.

Tom reached down and pulled her up. "You okay?"

"Just a little embarrassed."

Hand in hand they walked to his front porch. The light was on, the wreath was festive and the place seemed to be welcoming him home. There was something much more enticing about it than the usual bachelor lair.

She turned to face him and he was smiling down at her, waiting for her to make her move.

She put her arms around his waist and leaned her head back. "If you don't bend down a little I'm not going to be able to manage this," she told him.

He must've figured he'd teased her enough. He enfolded her in his arms so that she felt snug and safe and cherished, and then his lips met hers in a kiss of such warmth that she wanted to melt. She had been so programmed by Bobby's roughness, by his habit of equating affection with sex, that it took her a few moments to lose her guard and begin to relax.

It was only when her nose began to turn numb that she pulled away a little, and then it was to bury her face in his wool muffler. His arms tightened around her as his lips found her hair.

"Are you as surprised as I am?" he asked.

"It was only going to be a friendly kiss," she said, her lips smiling against his muffler.

"I'd say it was friendly."

She pulled away and looked up at him. "I wasn't expecting..."

"Neither was I."

Her arms loosened their grip on him and they ended up holding hands. "Well, I guess I'd better go. It's getting late."

"I guess you'd better. So, are you going to call my machine or am I going to call yours?"

"You really shouldn't be seeing me, should you? Because of Bobby being your client?"

"No, I really shouldn't."

"What're we going to do about it?"

"I don't know. We'll have to talk about it."

"Yes."

"Soon," he added.

"Yes, very soon."

About the last thing Holly had expected that Christmas season was to start falling in love.

Interlude

She dropped the finished chapter on the table where he was scarfing down his bucket of Kentucky Fried Chicken, then headed for the door.

"Where're you going?" he asked her.

"For a run."

"Now?"

"It makes me too nervous watching you read my chapter. Anyway, I could use it. I'm getting out of shape from sitting around watching TV all the time."

"Is that a complaint?"

She opened the door, then paused. "Well, I think I like sports as much as you do, but I hadn't anticipated a cable channel with sports twenty-four hours of each day."

"Isn't it great?"

"For a couch potato, maybe," she mumbled, going outside and closing the door behind her. She did a minimal amount of warming-up exercises, then set out at a slow jog for the beach where she thought she'd run in the sand and get the extra benefit to her calf muscles.

She wasn't getting any exercise anymore. Bobby had had a point with what he'd said about getting out of a warm bed every morning. During her first marriage it had been a relief to get up and out; this time it was turning out to be an impossibility. The last thing she wanted to do in the morning was extricate her warm limbs from his; it was all either of them could do to even make it to work in the morning.

She wouldn't mind running at night, although then she was so energized she had a problem falling asleep. But he objected to her running at night. He said he was worried about her out running alone, which was probably true, but she also knew he liked her on the couch beside him watching the games. And most of the time she wanted to be there. But her arms and legs were getting soft and she didn't like the way they looked. Once she had gotten used to having muscles, seeing arms and legs without them looked bad to her. She also felt better when she ran.

She wasn't pleased with the chapter she'd written and had overdone the part at her mother's house with everyone overeating, but she'd been upset at the time she wrote it and took it out on her writing.

It had started when he came home a few nights before and told her the results of his physical. The doctor had told him he was in perfect health and to keep doing whatever he'd been doing because he was doing something right.

So what could she say to that? If he was perfectly healthy and not an ounce overweight, she had no right to ask him to cut down on his eating. It was getting to her, though. It was getting to the point where she snapped at him at almost every meal. There were times she would have walked out, if she hadn't been so in love with him. And the problem was, love or not, she could foresee that happening some time in the future.

One day something in her would snap and she would pick up his plate of food and dump it over his head. She knew it was likely to happen because she'd thought about it so many times and come close a few.

He should never have married her. He deserved a woman like her mother who equated love with food and couldn't get enough of filling him up. He needed someone like himself, someone whose metabolism allowed constant binges with no weight gain in the process.

She was never going to be like that. A couple of times after her weight loss, when she was at her desired weight, she thought maybe it would be okay for her to eat normally if she didn't overdo it. She thought perhaps a piece of cake or a chocolate sundae wouldn't hurt anything. Both times she had been wrong. Not only had she gained, but once she had a taste of what she couldn't have, she lusted for more. And lust was the right word. During her entire marriage with Bobby food had taken the place of sex for her. Food, not sex, was what had given her pleasure.

At least that wasn't true today. Sex played a very strong part in their marriage, but still, more and more, she found herself also lusting for food.

She had a real problem and she didn't know what to do about it.

HE WAITED until he finished the chicken to read the chapter so he wouldn't get grease all over the pages. He was looking forward to reading them. What they were giving each other was a rare opportunity to look into the other's thoughts and learn things they might otherwise never have known.

He had come to realize she was more honest in revealing her feelings than he was. He was writing things as he remembered them, but his feelings hadn't come into it much. He'd try to be better at that. It wasn't fair when she got to the truths of the situations for him to skirt the truths and get on with the facts. It was also something she was sure to start calling him on anytime now.

Why was she out running? Why would anyone run if they didn't have to? He could see running around playing baseball, involving himself in some sport. But to run for no reason at all? It didn't make any sense to him. He knew there were people who did it, but he had never understood it. It seemed as pointless and boring to him as watching a track meet on TV.

He cleaned up the table, even carrying the bucket full of chicken bones out to the trash can in the garage so she wouldn't have to smell it in the kitchen. Then he washed his hands and carried the chapter into the living room.

The first part was a little boring. He paused in his reading for a moment to try to figure out why, then realized it was because he didn't appear in the first part. Well, there was ego for you! If he wasn't in it, was he going to want to read it? Probably not, but he'd read it anyway.

He began to read more carefully when he got to the part where she lied to her mother about seeing him. She had seen him, yes, but not in the way she led her mother to believe. He wondered if she always lied to her mother, and whether that meant she would lie to him. On the other hand, he lied to his mother on occasion. Didn't everyone? It probably didn't mean a thing.

Except that in the next part it did seem to mean something. He had always believed she had called him up and invited him to dinner because she had enjoyed his company. Now he was finding out it was only to get Bobby off her back. He had thought that perhaps their dinner out together hadn't been as bad as he had supposed it to be. That she had actually enjoyed herself and he had misconstrued it. But now he was finding out that she hadn't enjoyed it any more than he had. Although that really wasn't any reason to get mad at her. In fact, it made more sense.

Well, at least it hadn't come easy for her. She had found out it wasn't all that easy to call someone and ask them out. Sometimes it was damn difficult. He didn't know anyone who hadn't been turned down enough times so that he began to anticipate rejection every time even when he knew for a fact it was a sure thing.

He read on. The part about her family, the part where she gave their weights, wasn't fair. That was making fun of people. And the dinner? He couldn't remember them stuffing themselves like that. It was just a good dinner, that was all, and they had enjoyed it. What was the matter with enjoying a dinner? Just because she liked playing the martyr and starving herself to death, did that mean everyone should?

And thinking he was so nice just for acting the way anyone should act. What did she think he was going to do, remark on what a fat family she had? Sure they were fat. So what? There were thin people and fat people and that was just the way the world was. Were you supposed to look down on the half that was fatter than you? They were good people, and that was

what counted. Anyway, they didn't eat any more than
he did. It was a metabolism problem, that's all.

He was beginning to get angry until he got to the
part about their good-night kiss. Yeah, it had been
just like that. Of course she didn't know that after that
kiss it took all his self-control not to pick her up and
carry her into his house and make love to her. Or that
it took two cold showers and a couple of sandwiches
before he could calm down enough to sleep that night.

The kiss had been a real surprise. He had been having good feelings about her by then, but he hadn't
thought the good-night kiss was going to be anything
more than a formality. Well, it turned out to be a hell
of a lot more than that. That kiss had opened up feelings in him he hadn't even been aware of.

He heard the kitchen door open. It was a good thing
he had gotten to the kissing part before she got back
because it had put him in a better mood. And at least
when he finished talking to her about the chapter it
would end on an up note.

She came into the living room, standing tentatively
for a moment as though afraid of disturbing him.

"It's okay, I finished," he told her.

"Just a sec, let me get a towel," she said, and in a
minute she was back wiping the sweat off her face. She
looked as if she'd been running for her life.

"This was pretty interesting," he told her.

She took a seat as far away from his as possible. She
was still panting a little and it took her a moment to
speak. "I hope it didn't make you mad."

"If you were afraid of making me mad, why didn't
you fictionalize it?"

"I thought of that, but I didn't know how. It's so
much easier just to write from experience."

"Were you ever going to tell me you invited me out under false pretenses?"

"I didn't ask why you invited me out."

"I asked you for the usual reasons—because I was attracted, because I wanted to get to know you better."

"Because you didn't want to eat alone."

"That's a legitimate reason."

"If I hadn't thought you'd enjoy the dinner, though, I wouldn't have asked you. I could've avoided talk of Bobby by not going at all. Anyway, aren't you glad I did?"

He would've liked to argue that point, except he *was* glad. "Yeah, I'm glad," he admitted.

"If I hadn't, we wouldn't be here now."

He said, "The parts about 'weighing in at'..."

"Too graphic?"

"Too cruel. That's your family you're talking about."

"But those are their weights. It's not like I'm exaggerating."

"Still..."

"Look," she said. "Before we send the book out, I'll ask them if they mind. If they do, I'll leave it out. But I honestly don't think they'll mind."

"I guess that's all right, then."

"Anything else?"

"You make us sound like a bunch of pigs."

She was silent, avoiding his eyes.

"Never mind your family, is that the way you see me?"

"I don't get it. You saw that picture of me that night, the one in my wedding dress, and all you said was something about what a nice couple we made. Didn't you notice how fat I was?''

"Of course I noticed. I'm not blind."

"Didn't you care?"

"All I remember thinking at the time was how amazing I thought it was that you could've gotten so thin. It couldn't have been easy after being brought up on your mother's cooking."

"It wasn't easy, but you've never mentioned it once."

"You never brought the subject up."

She gave him an uneasy look. "Are we fighting?"

"No, we're just discussing something."

"Well? Don't you have any opinion about my once being fat?"

"What you're asking is, would I have been attracted to you when you were fat."

"No, I'm not asking that. I know you wouldn't have been. I wouldn't expect you to be. Sissy Spacek isn't fat."

"Look, it's like asking you if you would have been attracted to me if you'd first seen me in a club doing a comedy act."

"I might've been."

"Really?"

"I find that part of you very appealing."

"Meaning that there are parts you don't find so appealing."

"Look," she said, "I don't see any point in going into that again. Your doctor said you were okay, so what can I say?"

"You can say, 'Darling, can I get you anything? A beer? A sandwich? Some potato chips?'"

"Didn't you just eat a whole bucket of chicken?"

"I was trying to be funny." As usual, though, his audience wasn't amused. He wouldn't mind a beer, though. He should have brought one in with him so that he wouldn't have to make a special trip to the kitchen. He had the idea that she kept count of his trips to the kitchen.

He tried something he hadn't tried in a while. "Listen, why don't we both have a beer and relax?"

"You know I don't—"

"We're talking Miller Lite. The only thing a Lite is going to do to you is relax you." And maybe, he hoped, put her in a good mood.

He couldn't read the look on her face, but then she said, "Okay."

"You want a beer?"

"I said okay."

Chapter Six

"Did you have a good marriage?" Tom asked him.

Bobby tilted back in the chair and put his feet on the edge of Tom's desk. He'd been to the office so many times now he felt at home. "Until the last couple of years, it was damn good. I guess you could say it was perfect."

That wasn't what Tom wanted to hear. He wanted to be the perfect man for Holly; he didn't want to hear someone else got there first. "Tell me about it." He knew, deep down, that it was the man asking, not the lawyer. And he felt no guilt whatsoever.

"She was always there, you know? If I wanted something, she got it. If I needed something done, she was there to do it. She was different then. You've seen her, right? But she even looked different then. She was fat, sure, but I like a woman with a little meat on her. Now...I don't know, the way she looks, it turns me off. She always had a mouth on her, though."

Tom refused to admit to himself he was even asking it when he said, "Was your sex life good?"

"*Mine* was. Holly wasn't really into sex, if you know what I mean."

Tom felt noble about letting that one pass.

"She knew about the other women, but she never gave me a hard time about it. She understood I was a hot-blooded man, and..." He winked at Tom, who didn't return the wink.

"So you were unfaithful to her?"

"Hey, it wasn't like that," Bobby protested. "Listen, it wasn't me they went for, it was Elvis. I was never actually unfaithful to her. It was the Elvis part of me that had those women. Hell, I even had to talk like Elvis when I was with them. Maybe I even made love like Elvis, but who the hell'd know?"

Tom began to reassess the insanity plea.

BOBBY WAS IN TOM'S OFFICE for regular sessions now. He had refused to plead guilty and cut a deal at first, so that now that he was beginning to worry about winning in court, it was too late and Judith Green, the assistant DA assigned to the case, wouldn't even talk deals. Like Tom, she was looking for the case to add some pizzazz to her career.

"Get serious," Judith had said the last time Tom called her. "The first terrorist in Queens's history and you want to plea-bargain it down to simple assault? Tommy, this is one case the DA's office can't afford *not* to prosecute."

"Since when is an irate ex-husband a terrorist, Judy?" He'd been put off by her use of the diminutive and decided to reciprocate.

"When he holds an entire roomful of helpless women hostage, that's when."

"Helpless? Any one of them would've outweighed Bobby," said Tom, knowing as he said it what a cheap shot it was.

"Keep that line for court" had been all Judith would say.

Insanity was out. The act itself was insane, but Bobby wasn't. Extreme mental anguish was a possibility, but the problem with that was, why did he wait two years to make his move? He began to think that maybe he'd better get used to the possibility of losing his first big case. He sure would hate to lose it to Judith, though.

They had been in the same law class at St. John's, and not only was Judith four years younger than he was, she was twice as smart and ten times as ambitious. Her short-term ambition was to become the first female district attorney in New York. Her long-term ambition was to lock up the entire criminal element in the city. Her theory was that civil rights belonged only to the innocent.

Intelligence and ambition aside, she had also refused to go out with him. Tom couldn't take it all that personally, though, as she refused to date at all in law school—which probably had something to do with her graduating first in their class. And it wasn't as though he, or any of the other guys who tried, asked her out because of her looks and charm, although her looks were okay. They wanted to go out with her on the theory that some of that smartness would rub off on them.

A FEW NIGHTS BEFORE CHRISTMAS, Tom took Bobby up on his offer to comp him to a night at the Skylark Lounge. Holly was busy that night with her Weight Watchers meeting and Tom had been wanting to catch Bobby's act anyway. He had this idea that if he saw

Bobby impersonating Elvis, he'd understand his client better.

Anyway, there wasn't a Knicks game that night and he had nothing better to do. And he liked clubs. He kind of missed hanging out at comedy ones.

He was surprised at how prosperous the Skylark Lounge turned out to be. His first clue was the big parking lot, already full when he pulled in. His second clue was when he was asked whether he had a reservation.

"I'm a friend of Bobby's," he told the man, who looked more like a bouncer than a host.

"Everyone's a friend of Bobby's," he was told.

Tom looked past the man barring his way and saw that the place was packed. There wasn't an empty table or a place at the bar. In fact the bar was three deep. "I'll just stand at the bar," he told him.

"Suit yourself," the host said, and let him pass.

Tom looked over the place as he made his way through the crowd. Not only was the room enormous, with a bandstand and a large dance floor, but he also saw a sign over a door leading to an attached bowling alley. The place must make a mint. This was a few steps up from playing the comedy clubs.

He ordered a beer and looked over the crowd. He spotted Tiffany Benson in a far corner, but her table was filled with women. Then he spotted Judith. And there were two empty chairs at her table, the second chair taken up by Manny Cohn, also from their law class and also from the DA's office.

Carrying his beer, Tom made his way to their table. Without being asked, he pulled out a chair and seated himself, grinning at their surprise.

"Checking out the terrorist's act?" Tom asked them.

"And good evening to you, too," said Judith, looking none too pleased at him catching her there.

"Hey, Tommy, how's it going?" asked Manny.

"You in on the case, too?" Tom asked him.

Manny shook his head. "I'm just along for the ride. I was always a big Elvis fan."

Tom had always known there was something strange about Manny; now he knew what it was. "And you?" he asked Judith. "Are you a big Elvis fan, too?"

"By the time I ever saw Elvis," she said, "he was a fat, drugged-up old man. If we're talking about oldies, Barry Manilow's more my speed."

The guys both groaned at such lack of taste in a fellow attorney.

"So what're you going for?" Manny asked him. "Insanity?"

"An Elvis impersonator—what else could he plead?" asked Judith.

"I'm thinking of having it moved to federal court for political reasons," said Tom.

"Political?" asked Manny.

"Well, Judith insists on calling it an act of terrorism. Isn't that what the real terrorists do?"

"Domestic terrorism," said Judith. "Not being a feminist, however, you wouldn't know what I'm talking about."

"I figure it was political," said Tom. "The way I see it, the Elvis impersonator faction was going against the Weight Watchers faction."

The lights dimmed even more, some spotlights came on illuminating the bandstand, and Tom was relieved he wasn't going to have to carry his political theory any further. It was sounding stupid even to him.

The band started to play the introduction to "My Way," and the customers went crazy. There was whistling from the guys and screaming from the women, and then Bobby—or at least Tom assumed it was Bobby—came running out into the spotlight. His curly hair was slicked back, he had some phony sideburns and a stiff pompadour, his body was encased in white satin with enough sequins to light up the stage without the spotlight, and he was wearing honest-to-God electric-blue satin cowboy boots that matched his electric guitar.

"He really looks like him," said Judith.

"That's the easy part," said Manny. "Let's see if he sounds like him."

It was eerie, thought Tom as Bobby started to sing. It was like going back in time. He'd only seen Elvis in film clips, but if he didn't know the man was dead, he'd sure be fooled by Bobby. He had him down pat, even to the weird, wild look in his eyes. And the hips? Is that why the women were screaming? It was almost embarrassing to watch.

In the middle of his song, a woman, obviously overcome with emotion, ran up to the bandstand and held out her arms to Bobby. Without missing a beat of the song, Bobby leaned down and gave her a kiss. There was a lot more screaming at that, and a couple more women raced up to kiss the lips that sang the Elvis.

"We'll hold your seat for you any time you want to run up," Manny told Judith.

"Is the guy sexy, or have I had too much to drink?" she asked them.

"He's sexy," they both agreed.

Tom was feeling positively drab in comparison. If he had worn tight satin pants, would the women at the comedy clubs have besieged him? Would he have had groupies? Or was it just a long-gone Elvis they were going for?

The place went wild at the end of the song when Tiffany, all 285 pounds of her jiggling, ran up to get her kiss. It was longer than the others and when it was finished, Tom could see that Tiffany was almost faint with pleasure.

The band segued into "You Ain't Nothin' but a Hounddog," and now the famous Elvis hips really went into action. Bobby was shorter and better built than Elvis, and the tight pants left nothing to the imagination. Tom looked over at Judith and laughed out loud at her rapt expression.

"I think she's hooked," he said to Manny.

"Maybe I'll just have to take over the case," agreed Manny. "Obviously she can't successfully prosecute someone she wants to—"

"Shut up, Manny," said Judith. "I'm just amazed at the transformation, that's all." She tried to keep her eyes from Bobby, but, like the rest of them, she couldn't. Even Tom was finding something mesmerizing about him. He was a showman, that was for sure.

When the first show was over, instead of heading for his dressing room, Bobby came down off the bandstand and headed for their table. He had to kiss every woman he passed to get there, but he finally made it.

He stood glaring down at Tom. "What're you doing with the enemy?" he wanted to know.

"There weren't any empty tables."

"Hey, there's always a table for you," said Bobby, then turned his heavy-lidded gaze at Judith. "You enjoy the show, doll?"

Tom waited for the fireworks. No one called Judith "doll" and got away with it. It was enough to get a man killed.

Judith was cool, but only for a moment. That was the moment when Bobby reached down and smeared her lipstick all over her face.

Judith was still reeling from the kiss when Bobby moved on to another table.

Manny was laughing. "Was that the kind of research you had in mind?" he asked her.

"What an obnoxious pig," said Judith, but Tom noticed that her eyes were still following Bobby.

Tom followed her gaze and saw that Bobby was sitting at Tiffany's table, surrounded by adoring women.

Tom figured he'd settle for one woman, even if she wasn't adoring, and decided to leave the club and go home and call Holly.

"HOW WAS YOUR MEETING?" he asked her.

"It was good. They were still excited from last week. I guess they're all going to be witnesses."

"We can't talk about that," said Tom.

"Sorry. It's not like it's a secret, though. What'd you do tonight?"

For a split second he thought of not telling her. Then he remembered Tiffany's presence. "I went to the Skylark to catch Bobby's act."

"What'd you think of it?"

"I thought he was amazing."

"Were the women all going crazy?"

"I've never seen anything like it. Yeah, once. Once I saw Bowie in concert and the women were acting the same way."

"He eats it up."

Tom could understand that. What guy wouldn't? "I missed you tonight."

"Me too."

"Listen, I was wondering if you're busy Christmas Eve. Do you spend it with your family?"

"No, Christmas Day's the big day with us. Christmas Eve I usually wrap presents, watch TV."

"I have tickets to the Knicks game that night. I was wondering if you'd want to go."

"Are you kidding? I'd much rather watch the Knicks than watch *Miracle on 34th Street* for the hundredth time."

"Great!"

"What are you doing for Christmas, Tom? You said your family was going to be away."

"Nothing much."

"You mean you're not spending it with friends?"

"It's no big deal."

"It's a very big deal," said Holly. "And my family would love to have you join us."

"I wouldn't say no to your mom's cooking."

"And Tom?"

"Yeah?"

"No presents. If you want to bring something, bring Mom a box of candy."

"I got you something."

"Well, that's all right—I got you something, too. Let's exchange them Christmas Eve."

Tom was feeling really good when he hung up. The way things were going, it would probably be his best Christmas ever.

HE LET JOLENE OFF at noon Christmas Eve, after giving her a bonus and a pair of leather gloves. Then he carried the office Christmas tree home intact, decorations and all.

It looked good standing in front of one of the windows in his living room. He needed more, though. He needed some logs for the fireplace and some eggnog and other goodies to set out and he also needed to do a little last-minute Christmas shopping.

He wanted everything perfect. He wanted to invite Holly over after the game and, if things went as planned, he was hoping she'd still be there for breakfast on Christmas morning. He didn't think he was rushing things. He hoped he wasn't rushing things. They'd been out a few times now and the good-night kisses had progressed somewhat, and he felt now was the time for them to spend an entire night together. He was pretty sure she felt the same way, or as sure as you could be about something like that.

Of course she might prefer they stay at her place. He hoped not. There was something about the jungle effect of her place that turned him off. He was always expecting snipers to be lurking behind the plants. Plus, she only had a twin bed, and he had a king.

By the time he left to pick her up, he had the place looking perfect. There were clean sheets on the bed and clean towels in the bathroom. The logs were all set to be lit. The tree was on, and beneath it—giftwrapped—was his present to her. He had even hung two stockings from the mantel and filled them with candy and popcorn balls. The refrigerator held eggnog and all the makings of a big breakfast.

He dressed in clean jeans and a forest-green wool sweater, then decided to wear his brown leather bomber jacket that was lined in shearling. The temperature was supposed to do a nose-dive down to single digits and his car heater worked none too well.

When he picked Holly up, she came out of the trailer carrying an enormous, gift-wrapped object, which she carefully placed in the back seat of the car. Tom didn't ask "Is that for me?" because he was sure it was. What she'd be getting him that size, though, he couldn't figure out.

Tom started up the car and headed for Manhattan. After a few minutes, Holly said, "It's freezing in here."

"Something's wrong with my heater."

"Bring it by my office and I'll take a look at it for you."

"You fix cars?"

"I'm learning. I've got a lot of them to practice on."

Tom was impressed. The workings of cars were a complete mystery to him. "So how's business?"

"Not bad. It always picks up over the holidays. How about you?"

"Got a couple more clients for wills. I'm getting a reputation amongst the elderly of Queens as someone who draws up a terrific will."

"You don't sound enthusiastic."

"The only thing worse would be real estate closings, but at least they'd pay more."

When they got to the Garden, he parked in the garage on Thirty-first Street. As they walked over to the

Garden, a wind came off the Hudson and nearly blew them off the sidewalk. With the wind, it had to be twenty below.

They were stopped every two seconds by guys asking them, "Selling tickets? Anyone got tickets?" Even though tickets were still being sold at the box office, the street sellers never gave up. A lot of people were asking for change, too, more than Tom had ever seen. He reached into his pockets and gave what he had, thankful he wasn't living on the street in weather like this—although they'd all eventually head for Penn Station, where at least they'd be out of the wind.

Inside the Garden, only the rowdy fans seemed to be out on Christmas Eve. Tom got himself a beer, got a tea for Holly, who seemed to need warming up, and then they found their seats. They were surrounded by a group of teenagers, the shortest of whom was well over six feet, and Tom had the feeling they were high school basketball players.

"I've never had seats this good," said Holly.

"You're in luck—I have season tickets."

"To all the games?"

"All of them."

Holly gave a sigh of contentment. She was looking good in a huge, light blue woolly sweater with a picture of a koala bear knit right into it, black leather pants and black boots. He thought it was the first time he'd seen her in anything but pink.

The Knicks were amazing that night, beating the 76ers in overtime with Patrick Ewing scoring the winning points. Afterward Holly and Tom stopped in Beafsteak Charlie's for a late dinner before heading back to Queens.

When they got to his house, Tom hung up their coats, then got a fire going in the fireplace.

"You have a Christmas tree," said Holly.

"I brought it home from the office."

"That's nice. I never get a tree. It doesn't seem to fit in with all the plants."

"You're welcome to enjoy mine."

"You even have stockings! Two of them?"

"One's for you."

Holly put the package she had been carrying under the tree, then kicked off her boots and curled up on the couch.

"How about some eggnog?" he asked her.

She seemed to consider that for a minute, then said, "Sure, why not?"

He brought in the eggnog and also the platter of hors d'oeuvres he'd had made up at the deli. He saw her eyes widen as he set the platter on the coffee table.

"You really went to a lot of trouble," she said.

"Listen, this is Christmas Eve." He went over to the stereo and tuned the radio to a station that was playing continuous Christmas music. Had Elvis recorded any Christmas songs? He hoped not; he didn't want to be reminded of Bobby.

"Open your present," said Holly, pointing to it under the tree.

"Now?"

"Yes. I can't wait for you to see it."

He'd been wondering about that odd shape all night. "Only if you open yours."

"You first," she said, getting up off the couch and going over to the tree. She picked up the package and handed it to him. It was heavy and hard and he faked having a hard time holding on to it.

"Be careful," she warned him. "It's breakable."

Tom tore apart the paper and then stared at it with wonder. "Where did you find it? I've looked all over for one of these."

"I have connections," said Holly, grinning at him.

"This is my brand," he told her.

"I know."

Tom carried it over and set it on a table, then plugged it into an outlet. In a moment, "Miller Lite" was flashing on and off in colored neon lights.

He gave her a hug. "That's the most perfect present I ever received. I figured I was going to get a sweater."

"Give me credit for a little imagination."

"I'm afraid I wasn't nearly as imaginative. I mean, I could've gotten you another plant for that jungle of yours, but I figured you didn't have room. Then I thought of parakeets."

"Parakeets?"

"You know, those little brightly colored birds."

"I know what they are, but why in the world would you think of parakeets?"

"I just thought they'd look good flying around in that jungle."

"Well, I'm glad you didn't get them. I don't like birds much."

"Then I thought of getting you a VCR."

"I don't want a VCR. If I don't have time to watch something while it's on, I don't have time later, either."

"You can always rent movies."

"I'd rather see them at the theater."

"Well, that's okay, because I didn't get you a VCR." He had a feeling she thought he was trying to prolong the suspense, which wasn't it at all. The truth of the matter was, he was beginning to think what he got her was too personal. She might be offended. She might even think he was being pretentious. That was why he had thrown in those other ideas he had had, so she wouldn't think what he got her was the only thing he could think of.

"Tom, I'm going to like it whatever it is, so quit worrying about it."

"I'm not so sure."

"Well, why don't you get it over with?"

Feeling as though he was up against something traumatic now, Tom went over and got the small package from under the tree and handed it to her. The store had gift-wrapped it for him in silver paper and a gold bow. He hoped she wouldn't think that was his taste in wrapping paper. He preferred brightly colored paper with Santa Clauses on it.

"It's too pretty to open," she said, carefully removing the ribbon and then the paper.

She looked a little nervous. Well, since it was obviously a jewelry box, maybe she thought he'd jumped the gun and bought her a diamond ring. He wished she knew him well enough to know he wouldn't do something as potentially embarrassing as that.

She lifted the lid and appeared to turn pale. He had shocked her, which was the last thing in the world he wanted to do.

"You can always return them," he said.

She was looking down at the emerald earrings and shaking her head.

"I guess they're not the kind of thing you'd wear."

She was lifting one out and looking at it.

"Holly, I'm feeling really stupid. Would you say something?"

She looked over at him. "You gave me emerald earrings?"

"I thought of diamonds, but then I saw those and the color was so great—"

"They're incredible."

"Does that mean you like them? You don't have to be polite, you know."

"Like them? No one's ever given me such a beautiful gift in my whole life. You know what Bobby's biggest Christmas present to me was? A vacuum cleaner."

"If you'd rather have another color—"

"Another *color*? These are emeralds! Why on earth would I want another color?"

"I was afraid you'd think they were a little pretentious?"

She grinned at him. "You think I mind being a little pretentious? Everyone'll die when they see me walking around with emerald earrings." She began to fit one of the studs into her ear, then turned it for him to see. "Do they look gorgeous?"

"You looked gorgeous already."

She put the other one in, then said, "Lead me to the nearest mirror."

She followed him into the bedroom where he had a mirror over his dresser. He turned on the overhead light so she could get a good look at herself. She turned this way and that, admiring the earrings, the grin never leaving her face. Then she turned around and her gaze took in the bedroom.

"Are you always this neat?" she asked him.

"I cleaned up today."

Her eyes took in the king-size bed with the small TV set on a cart at the end of it, the navy-blue bedspread that matched one of the stripes in the wallpaper he had hung himself, and the Leroy Neiman basketball print he had hanging over the bed. "This is very nice," she said.

"I got tired of furnished apartments."

She moved closer to him and gave him a kiss. "Thank you. I'm so pleased with these."

"I'm glad," he said. There was a silence and he finally broke it up by saying, "How about another eggnog?"

"I wouldn't mind," she said, following him out to the kitchen.

When they were back on the couch with their drinks, the neon light flashing, her emeralds catching the light and also flashing, he decided to make his move. If not now, when?

"I was thinking," he said, "would you want to spend the night?"

"Oh, good, I was hoping I wouldn't have to go back out in the cold."

He wasn't sure about that answer. It wasn't that he didn't like it, it was more that he wasn't positive she had understood him correctly.

He said, "I wasn't offering you the guest room, you understand."

She smiled at him. "That's even better."

"This isn't a casual offer," he tried to explain. "What I mean is, I wouldn't ask just anyone to spend the night with me on Christmas Eve." That came out sounding all wrong. It made it sound as though any other night he would.

"You don't have to explain, Tom. I feel exactly the same way."

"Exactly?"

She moved over next to him and circled his waist with her arm. "Exactly."

Over the radio came, "Merry Christmas to all, and to all a good-night."

Interlude

She turned astonished eyes from the pages to his face. "You left out the sex," she said, accusation in her voice.

"The sex?"

"You have me circling your waist with my arm, and then you *end* it? With the last line of "The Night Before Christmas" that wouldn't even be playing on the radio? I don't believe you even remember what was playing on the radio."

"Of course I don't, do you?"

She gave a sigh of exasperation. "That's beside the point. The point is, where's the sex?"

"There's such a thing as privacy, isn't there?"

"Not in these books, there's not. Come on, you spend pages describing the Christmas presents we exchanged, and then, just when it's getting interesting, you fade out."

"How about if I end it with him carrying her into the bedroom?"

"You didn't carry me into the bedroom."

"No, but it sounds more interesting. More romantic."

"It sounds ridiculously outdated. I think you watch too many old movies."

"What should he do, drag her into the bedroom?"

"Why? Because you think that makes a good end to your chapter? The point is, it shouldn't end there. It doesn't matter how they get to the bedroom. They can *walk* to the bedroom. Just get them there and then describe what happened."

"Are you serious?"

"You have it all set up. You have him hoping that she'll spend the night. You even have him putting clean sheets on the bed. You can't just leave it at that and expect the readers to use their imagination. They're not used to using their imaginations—it's all spelled out for them these days."

He got up and went out to the kitchen, returning with an opened beer in his hand. "Forget it, I'm not writing sex."

"It's not just sex, it's love. It should be a love scene. These books are called romances, you know."

"There's no way I can do that."

"Just a couple of pages, that's all I'm asking."

"No."

"Why not? If you can describe everything else in such detail, why can't you write the love scene?"

"I'd be embarrassed to death, that's why. There's no way I could write that stuff."

"I'll bet you could've written a play-by-play description of the Knicks game that night."

"But I didn't, did I? And you know why? Because I didn't think it belonged in the book. And I don't think sex does, either."

She began to tap her foot on the floor in a way that was guaranteed to drive him nuts. "I wasn't going to mention this," she said, a dangerous look in her eyes. "I wasn't going to pull that chapter apart paragraph by paragraph. But I'd be interested in knowing one thing. Since you're so hesitant about using anything having to do with sex in the book, just why did you ask Bobby about our sex life?"

"I knew you were going to get on me about that."

"I wasn't, but I am now. And don't tell me it was something you had to know in order to defend him."

He managed to look sheepish and contrite at the same time. "You really want to know?"

"I certainly do."

"I was jealous, that's why."

"Jealous of Bobby?"

"You were married to him, weren't you? And the guy's pretty sexy, you've got to admit."

"Maybe your idea of sexy—not mine."

"What's your idea of sexy?"

"You. Which you should know without my telling you. That night—Christmas Eve—the night you refuse to describe. Well, that was the way I always thought it should be, but up until then it never had been."

He said, "You never told me that."

"Well, it looks as though we don't tell each other a lot of things."

"I always figured you compared me to Bobby."

"Believe me, there's no comparison. Except that Bobby wouldn't hesitate to put it down in writing."

He nodded. "Well, that's the difference between us. I hesitate."

"Well, it's not fair. That's the first time they make love. Everyone's going to be dying to know how it turned out, and you just plain leave it out."

"I've got a great idea," he said. "You can put it in the next chapter."

"That's too late. That's anticlimactic."

"You can have them waking up Christmas morning and making love again."

"We did."

"I know we did."

"But that's the second time. The readers are going to want to read about the first."

"Look, you want to go to a movie?"

Her foot began tapping again. "Quit changing the subject. I think we have to settle this."

"As far as I'm concerned, it's settled."

With a sneaky little smile on her face, she moved across the room and sat next to him on the couch. "What if I help you?"

"Go ahead, be my guest. The typewriter's all yours."

"I didn't say I'd write it. I said I'd help you."

"I told you, I'm not doing it. And sitting next to me like that isn't going to change my mind."

She inched over a little closer and pulled his arm around her. "How did it start, anyway? How *did* we get to the bedroom?"

"You mean you don't remember?"

"Not exactly."

"You practically dragged me in there."

"I did not!"

"What happened was, we started kissing—"

"I remember that."

"And then you started pulling my clothes off—"

She threw his arm off her shoulder. "That's not the way I remember it!"

"Hey, I was only joking. As I recall, one thing led to another, and we both decided to continue it in bed."

"That's what I mean. You can't just say 'one thing led to another.' You have to describe it in detail."

"Look, why don't we go to a movie and talk about this afterward."

"No."

He put his arm back around her. "Okay, you want the details? I slipped my hands up under your sweater and began to feel you."

"*Feel* me? That sounds awful."

"What do you want me to say? I mean, I'm not even sure what words you're allowed to use in these books."

"Caress would be a good word. You began to slowly caress my breasts."

"You telling me you can use *breasts*?"

"Why not? It's a perfectly good word. And far preferable to some others I can think of."

"I can't wait to hear what word you use when you caress *me*."

"Don't worry, we'll think of a nice euphemism."

"I'm not sure exactly what happened, but I know we ended up lying down on the couch."

"With me on top."

He nodded. "Right."

"And I think it was pretty soon after that we went to the bedroom."

"And you immediately disappeared into the bathroom."

She said, "We can leave that out and just get to the good part."

"Okay, so we're in bed—"

"We have to get undressed first."

He looked a little uneasy. "What do we do then, describe the bodies?"

"Of course."

"No way. This is really getting embarrassing. I mean, what if someone we know reads this book?"

"If we get it published, I'm going to make sure that *everyone* we know reads it."

"Forget the bodies."

"I don't know what you're worried about," she said, "you happen to have a great body. In fact I remember being surprised since I knew you didn't work out."

"Can't we have her thinking what a great body he has without actually describing it?"

She shrugged. "I guess you're right. There's really no need to describe our bodies. At that point they can just picture Sissy Spacek and Jeff Bridges."

"A *thinner* Jeff Bridges," he reminded her.

"Okay, so we're in bed—"

"And we pull up the covers and fade out."

She chuckled. "I'm afraid not. Now we start going into detail."

"Can you actually remember the details?"

"The important ones."

"Well, yeah, I can remember those."

"We need more, though," she said. "We need things like the scent of her perfume and the texture of the sheets against their naked, writhing bodies, and the way his swollen tongue filled her mouth—"

"Give me a break!"

"Those things are important. They add atmosphere."

"Can we take these one at a time? In the first place, I've never noticed you wearing perfume. Maybe my sense of smell isn't so great, but—"

"You're right, I don't. It makes me sneeze. If I even get into an elevator with a woman wearing perfume, I sneeze. I think it's an allergy."

"So, we don't need the perfume."

"You were wearing something, though, I remember."

"Yeah. Men's cologne. But I didn't put it on until we got home. I mean, I don't go to a basketball game wearing cologne."

"Well, you didn't have to wear it for me, either. I kept feeling like I was going to sneeze."

He burst out laughing. "Well, that's sure romantic."

"I think it's sweet you put it on, though. I popped a breath mint in my mouth when I went into the bathroom."

"I noticed."

"You did?"

"Well, before you went in you tasted like eggnog, and when you came out you tasted of spearmint."

"As I recall, your bedroom smelled like pine, but I guess that was from the Christmas tree."

He shook his head. "No, that was from a spray. I sprayed the whole house before you came over. The air was stale, and it was too cold to open the windows. We could mention a pine scent, I guess."

"Pine scent isn't romantic unless you're making love in the woods."

"Okay, so what about the sheets? How do you describe the texture of cotton?"

She smiled. "We'll make them satin. Satin sheets always sound so sexy."

"Forget it!"

"What have you got against satin sheets?"

"I'm not the kind of guy who would run out and buy satin sheets in case the woman I want to make love to might want to write a book about it some day."

"Red satin. That's kind of Christmasy."

"No way," he said. "Satin sheets sound sleazy. Would you really like some guy who had satin sheets on his bed?"

"I guess not."

"Damn right! Now if you had them, that'd be different."

"I don't like the feel of satin."

"Then what're we arguing about? What was that last thing? My swollen tongue? I don't know where you're coming from with that, but I don't think my tongue suddenly becomes swollen when I kiss."

She gave him a mystified look. "You know something? I keep reading that in books, about swollen tongues, but I don't know what they're talking about, either. As I recall, your tongue felt perfectly normal."

He nodded his head once. "Okay. So we've got them in bed, there's a fresh scent in the air, the cotton sheets are cool to their touch, and his nonswollen tongue is in her mouth. Now what happens?"

"That just doesn't sound right."

"It sounds perfectly rational to me."

"I wasn't even wearing a lacy negligee."

"I would have been pretty surprised if you had been carrying one in your handbag to the basketball game."

"Why not? I was carrying a few other things in my handbag."

"Like what?"

"Just things. Like a toothbrush."

"You went out on a date with me carrying a toothbrush?"

"Is that any different than your changing the sheets?"

He grinned. "I guess not. Okay, you can have a lace negligee in your handbag if you want."

"When have you ever seen me in a lace negligee?"

"I haven't."

"I don't even own one. If I had put anything in my handbag to sleep in, it would have been flannel pajamas, and that doesn't sound romantic."

"So what do we do? Stick to naked bodies?"

She squeezed his hand. "You can't get much sexier than that."

He sighed in contemplation. "I guess not."

"Except for my earrings. I was naked except for the flashing green emeralds in my pearly white earlobes."

"I remember scratching my hand on them a couple of times."

"I can remember your rough chin scratching me a couple of times."

He grinned at her. "Where?"

"You know where."

"If you can't say it, how are you going to be able to write it?"

She said, "His rugged chin sent chills along her pearly white limbs."

He did a double-take. "What's with this 'pearly white' business? You make yourself sound like an albino."

"You like ivory better?"

"I like freckled better. Your thighs are freckled."

"Heroines don't have freckled thighs. Anyway, I don't see you objecting to the part about your rugged chin."

"My chin wasn't so bad. I shaved right before you came over."

"And I used freckle remover on my thighs."

He gave her a look, then realized she was kidding. "Okay. What comes next?"

"As I recall, most of the foreplay took place in the living room."

"That's the way I remember it."

"Which means we pretty much got right down to business in the bedroom."

He nodded. "Is that what you say? 'Got down to business'?"

"No, of course not."

"What do you say?"

"Well . . . maybe we should say you were on top."

"But I wasn't."

"Yes, but it sounds better."

"I was on top the second time."

"Okay, so you're straddling me and I'm hanging on to your muscular shoulders—"

He gave a pleased smile. "You like my shoulders?"

"I like your shoulders fine. They're not particularly muscular, but then you're not a ditch digger, are you?"

"And then what happens?"

"And then we do it."

"Yes, I know, but is that all you say? 'They *did* it'?"

"No, you say something like, 'He plunged his manhood into the font of her womanhood.'" She was laughing by the time she finished saying it.

"You have to use words like that?"

She nodded, laughing so hard tears were streaming out of her eyes.

"Forget it. I'm going to be the laughingstock of the Queens court system if this ever gets out."

She wiped her eyes as her laughter died down. "You're right. My clients would laugh me out of town. Either that or they'd start making remarks about the font of my womanhood."

"So we just do a fade-out?"

"I guess so. It seems like a cop-out, but I don't think I could write it, either."

"It's funny, though," he said. "All this talk about it, it's kind of gotten me in the mood."

"Me, too."

He pulled her closer. "There's no reason why we have to go to a movie tonight."

"We could just stay home," she agreed, nuzzling his chest with her nose.

"We could just go to bed and watch TV."

She nodded. "What's on?"

"Does it matter?"

She got up off the couch and reached for his hand. "With your manhood and my womanhood, who needs TV?"

Chapter Seven

After one of the coldest, snowiest Decembers on record, it unaccountably warmed up on Christmas Day. The sun came out, the snow began to turn to slush, and Holly woke up to a very warm bed.

She turned and looked at Tom's clock radio. It was flashing 11:04 in bright red letters. Her mother was expecting them around one. Holly's family favored an early Christmas dinner. That way they could also have a Christmas supper of leftovers.

Okay, that gave them almost two hours before they had to be there. Say forty minutes to get dressed, twenty minutes for the drive, that left about fifty-six minutes to make love. Or, perhaps they could manage to get ready in thirty minutes—it would save time if they showered together; going over the speed limit slightly he might be able to cut five minutes off the driving time; and that would leave... She couldn't quite figure it out in her head, but she knew it would add to their lovemaking time. It was a good thing they had opened their presents the night before.

But before they could even begin to make love, she had to wake him up. She rolled over to face him and gave him a kiss on his slightly parted mouth from which little puffs of breath were being emitted. "Merry Christmas," she said.

He replied in something that sounded like a foreign language.

She rolled halfway onto his body, one of her legs winding around his. "Merry Christmas, Tom," she said a little louder.

This time one of his eyes opened, eyed her dubiously, and closed again. All right, so they hadn't gotten much sleep. That wasn't any reason to sleep away Christmas Day.

She rolled back onto her side of his bed, and began to sing "I Heard the Bells on Christmas Day." She didn't know why she picked that particular song out of all the Christmas songs she knew, perhaps she had heard it on the radio the night before and the melody had stayed in her head.

She had only gotten a few bars into it when both of his eyes opened. "You've got to be kidding," he groaned.

"Merry Christmas," she said in what she hoped was a cheery manner. Maybe he was a grump in the morning. Maybe she had to be careful.

The eyes closed and what sounded suspiciously like a snore was heard.

Well, perhaps actions did after all speak more loudly than words. She rolled back over to his part of the very large bed, wrapped her warm body around his warm body, and hugged him close to her.

The snores stopped and she heard a noise that sounded like it had something to do with pleasure.

She began to move her body just a little bit. Nothing flagrant, just a steady, friendly sort of movement, just enough to get a rise out of him. Out of his manhood.

Tom responded, wrapping his arms firmly around her, and then his body began to move beneath hers. She thought he must be awake, even though his eyes were still closed, because people couldn't do what they were now doing when they were asleep, could they?

Their movements became a little stronger, a little more coordinated. Their mouths met and locked, and then she was throwing the covers back and abandoning herself to the moment and the movement and all the pleasure she was deriving from that movement, and when he finally did open his eyes, it was at the very last moment possible and he was looking at her with the same kind of stunned excitement that she was feeling herself.

And then, of course, it was another few moments before either of them could speak.

"Were you singing before?" he asked her.

"I was trying to wake you up."

"Your second idea was a lot better."

"We only have about an hour and a half before we have to be at my mother's."

He abruptly sat up. "It's that late?"

"Well, we were up pretty late."

He smiled down at her. "We were, weren't we? For a while there, I thought I could stay up all night, but at some point I must've conked out."

"We both did," said Holly.

He moved his legs off the bed, then stood up. "Listen, take a shower, get dressed, do whatever you have to do, but stay out of the kitchen. I'm fixing you my Christmas breakfast special."

Breakfast? An hour before dinner? "But we'll be eating at my mother's," she reminded him.

"Not breakfast," he said, picking up his jeans off the floor and putting them on. "You can't start off a day without breakfast."

Holly couldn't argue with that as Weight Watchers had the same philosophy. Nevertheless, two meals within an hour of each other wasn't their mode of eating, either.

"I'm not really hungry," said Holly.

He looked aghast. "That didn't work up an appetite for you?"

It had worked up an appetite for more of the same, but not for breakfast. She was too shy to say that, though, and by the time she thought of some other argument, he was out of the room, and then the next thing she heard were kitchen noises.

Instead of the red wool Christmas dress she had planned to wear, Holly showed up in the kitchen fifteen minutes later in the same clothes she had worn the night before. They were perfectly all right and besides they would save a lot of time if she didn't have to stop off at the trailer and change.

Tom had a very nice kitchen table under a window that looked out over his yard. The tabletop was made of white tiles surrounded by wood and she had admired it the first time she saw it. Today, however, the white tiles were completely obscured by plate after plate of food, and there wasn't anything about it she admired.

There were scrambled eggs—what looked like dozens of scrambled eggs. There was a pound or two of bacon. There were home fries made with onions and green pepper. There was a coffee cake. Oh, God, there was a cinnamon raisin coffee cake, the very same kind she used to be addicted to. Was still addicted to, if the way her eyes were fastened on it was any indication.

"Tom, is all this for us?"

"Don't be shy—help yourself. The juice is in the pitcher and I'll have the coffee ready in a minute."

What was the very worst that could happen if she refused to eat? The answer wasn't palatable. Neither was the food, but if she didn't eat any of her mother's dinner, maybe she'd be okay. There was just no way she could make love to him all night and then refuse the breakfast he made for her.

Holly sat down. She took what she reckoned to be an ounce of scrambled eggs onto her plate. She picked up two slices of bacon and transferred them to the empty space beside her eggs. She totally ignored the home fries, although their smell alone was driving her up the wall. She poured herself a half glass of orange juice. And, dear God, let her have the strength to resist the coffee cake.

Tom brought two steaming cups of coffee over to the table and took the seat across from her. "I bet you didn't know I could cook," he said.

"I was sure you could. Anyone who lives alone in a house can probably cook for himself."

Fortunately he didn't remark on the small amounts of food on her plate. She found that by eating very slowly, she still had some left by the time he was helping himself to thirds.

"Have some more," he said to her.

"I'm stuffed," said Holly, pushing her chair back from the table just a smidgeon.

"Not going to have any of that coffee cake? I heated it up in the oven."

Holly eyed it with longing. With more than long-ing, with outright lust. "I'm allergic to cinnamon," she said, which wasn't a lie at all. She was definitely allergic to cinnamon. And sugar.

Tom cut himself a good quarter of the coffee cake and bit into it. Holly went a little crazy for a moment. With no remorse at all, she could have reached across the table, strangled him and taken the cake for her-self. If she stopped to think about it, that would make her just as crazy as Bobby holding them all hostage.

"You okay?" asked Tom.

"I'm great."

He smiled. "Me too. I've never felt better in my life. I'm crazy in love with you, you know."

"I'm crazy in love with you, too," she said, and his smile grew wider. For a fleeting moment, she won-dered if he would love her if she were fat. But that really wasn't the point, was it? She wouldn't love her-self if she were fat.

HOLLY'S MOTHER loved the painting and made Pee Wee get a hammer and some nails and put it up on the wall before they ate dinner. She also loved the bonus check Holly had given her from the business.

Tiffany was ecstatic over the twenty-five assorted paperback romances Holly had picked out for her for Christmas. The fact that Holly had read them first didn't count; they were Tiffany's to keep and read again.

Pee Wee was speechless over her gift to him, but whether out of joy or dismay she couldn't tell. She had a feeling, though, it was dismay. Holly had bought him a bench and weights for Christmas. If he wouldn't stop eating, maybe he could at least turn some of that fat into muscle.

Tom's four-pound box of chocolates for Marilyn was quickly devoured.

In the kitchen, her mother said, "What are those green things on your ears?"

"Emeralds," said Holly, pushing her hair back so that Marilyn and Tiffany could get a look at them. "Tom gave them to me for Christmas."

"Tom?" asked her mother. "The same Tom who last time I saw him there was nothing between you two?"

"I thought he was just a friend," said Tiffany.

"I've been seeing a lot more of him," said Holly.

"I would say so," said her mother. "Emeralds sound rather serious."

"They must be half a carat," said Tiffany.

"It's pretty serious," admitted Holly.

Her mother, who had always been partial to Bobby, surprised her. "Well, that's not a bad thing, if you ask me."

"Does Bobby know about this?" asked Tiffany.

"No, and don't tell him. Tom is his lawyer."

There was a silence, and then Marilyn said, "Is that legal, you two seeing each other?"

"We don't discuss the case," said Holly. "And Tom would always do what was best for his client."

"I'm sure he would," said Marilyn. "He seems real ethical to me."

"Maybe Bobby wouldn't care," said Tiffany, but that was so patently ridiculous an idea, no one even answered her.

DINNER WAS SOMETHING of a horror. Tom ate like a man starving to death rather than a man who had just consumed enough breakfast for an army platoon. The rest of her family followed suit, of course. Holly ate a minuscule portion of everything to keep the peace on Christmas.

Holly knew of other families who waited on dessert. Who cleaned off the table and gave their stomachs a rest, and then, maybe an hour or so later, served dessert. Not hers. No one in her family could ever wait for dessert. Instead, they adjourned to the living room for dessert since the dining room table was now covered with dirty dishes.

After dessert, Pee Wee must have figured his strength was up enough to tackle the weights. "Want to show me how to use those?" he asked Holly.

"Pee Wee, you should wait at least an hour after you eat." Not that an hour ever went by wherein something wasn't eaten by Pee Wee.

"We could all take a walk, though," said Holly, thinking it might be almost as good as a run. "It's nice out, really warm. And we could look at everyone's Christmas decorations."

That was voted down unanimously. Instead they watched *Raiders of the Lost Ark*, which was Pee Wee's favorite movie and which Tiffany had given him for Christmas.

Indiana Jones was just whipping out his gun to shoot the man with the knife when the doorbell rang. Pee Wee put the VCR on hold and went to answer it. When he came back, he wasn't alone.

"Oh, my God," said Holly, seeing a smiling Bobby loaded down with presents.

Then Bobby caught sight of Tom, and the smile was dropped as fast as the packages. "What's going on here?" asked Bobby.

"Merry Christmas, dear," said Marilyn, running to get him a piece of pie.

"Merry Christmas, Bobby," said Tiffany, looking from him to Holly in fear.

"Hey, Bobby," said Tom.

Bobby's smooth jaw began to twitch. "Hey, Bobby? Is that all you have to say to me? What I'd like to know is, what the hell my lawyer's doing here?"

"He's with me," said Holly.

There was a shocked silence, broken only by Marilyn coming back into the room and handing Bobby a piece of pie. For the first time in history Bobby ignored a piece of Marilyn's pie, setting it down on a table and glaring at Holly.

"What do you mean, with you?"

"I invited him," said Holly.

"Let me get this straight," said Bobby. "Are you two friends?"

"We met when she asked me to see you in jail," said Tom.

"And you've been meeting ever since?"

Tom nodded.

"In other words," said Bobby, "my lawyer, who's supposed to be defending me, is consorting with the enemy?"

"I'm not your enemy," said Holly.

"Oh? Does that mean you're not going to testify against me?"

Since it didn't mean that at all, Holly kept silent. Bobby turned his glare on Tom. "Well, let me tell you something, Mr. Hotshot Attorney. The way I see it, you got two choices. You can either stop seeing Holly or you can get the hell off my case. Do I make myself clear?"

"In that case," Tom started to say, but Holly put her hand on his arm.

"Can he have a little time to think it over?" Holly asked Bobby.

Bobby, a magnanimous smile on his face, said, "Of course. Would I be unfair about this? He has until tomorrow morning at ten." And with that, Bobby made his exit. It was rather like the exit he made when impersonating Elvis, but no one saw the humor in that except Holly, and she didn't feel like laughing.

"I knew there'd be trouble when you told me he was Bobby's lawyer," said Marilyn.

"Poor Bobby," said Tiffany. "He didn't even get to eat the pie."

"Can we watch the rest of the movie now?" asked Pee Wee.

"Tom and I are going downstairs to shoot some pool," said Holly. "We need to talk alone."

"There's nothing to talk about," said Tom when they got down to the basement. "I'm getting off the case."

"No, you're not," said Holly. "Dropping his case now is not fair to Bobby and it's not fair to you."

"Don't worry about being fair to me. I'd much rather have you than have a good case."

"But you can have me anyway once the trial is over."

"You're not talking me out of it, Holly."

"Aren't there some kind of ethics involved here, Tom? You took his case and then knowingly got involved with one of the witnesses against him. Now I know you wouldn't let that influence you, but would the judge feel the same way?''

"He'd call it a conflict of interest."

"And it is. But if Bobby has to find another lawyer now, and that other lawyer loses his case, we're going to be forever blamed for it."

"I should never have taken it."

"If you hadn't, we probably wouldn't be together now."

"I'm still not convinced."

"Then do it for me, okay? The thing is, this is happening so fast between us I'm getting a little scared. It was fast with Bobby, too, and it turned out disastrously. We can cool it for a while, and then when Bobby's case is decided one way or another, we'll know for sure what we want."

"I know for sure now," said Tom.

"I think I do, too. But I've been wrong before. Please, Tom, do it for me. If we really love each other, nothing will change."

Tom still looked unsure.

"No, forget that," said Holly. "I'm not giving you a choice. I need some time to think and I don't want to see you until after the trial. I haven't even known you that long and now I'm wearing your emeralds and we've made love and I feel like I'm on a merry-go-round and I need to slow down."

"I knew it was too good to last."

"That's the point, Tom. If it's that good, it will last. If it's not, then we might as well find out now."

Tom gave her a wry smile. "Now you make me wish I had forgotten about breakfast this morning."

It was nice to know, at least, that some things were more important to him than food.

She wondered how much of what she'd said to him was true and how much was manufactured on the spot. She did feel strongly that he shouldn't desert his client at this point, but her bid for time wasn't something she would have brought up without Bobby's intervention. But maybe it was a good idea. She had rushed into marriage with Bobby, and this time, when it felt so good, so right, maybe she shouldn't be as rash. She'd miss him dreadfully, though.

She thought about running into his arms for one last kiss, but then decided against it. Kissing him was just like eating cinnamon raisin coffee cake: one taste was never enough.

Interlude

She finished her chapter a day early that week and he took it to the office with him on Friday to read. She was nervous all day, wondering if he'd call her and have something he couldn't wait to say about it, but all the phone calls were business that day.

At first she was relieved. But as the day progressed she began to get paranoid. He always called her during the day. Was he mad at her? Weren't they speaking?

Finally, just before she locked up for the day, she called his office. And then, of course, found out he had been in court all day, which she had forgotten about.

She got home before him and started her dinner. Their eating and cooking arrangements were somewhat unique. In the refrigerator, his beer cans took up all of the door compartments; her fresh vegetables took up both drawers; her one carton of skim milk shared the top shelf with bottles of every soft drink full of sugar known to man; the other three shelves held his bacon and eggs and sausages and mayonnaise and bologna and cheese; the freezer was about evenly divided between his pizzas and candy bars and ice cream and her Weight Watchers frozen dinners.

They each cooked his or her own meal. She had cold cereal and a banana for breakfast; he had half the given contents of the refrigerator. They both ate lunch out. For dinner, they generally cooked side by side. Or rather she cooked her frozen dinner and prepared her salad and he nibbled on a sandwich while his pizza or spaghetti or whatever was cooking. He had already consumed more than she ate for dinner before he even sat down to eat.

Dessert was the hardest to bear. She would eat half a cup of a diet pudding while he brought an entire package of cookies to the table and consumed them. Sometimes he ate a pint of ice cream along with them. Occasionally he had the bad manners to stop at a bakery on the way home, but on those days she made excuses to flee the kitchen before he got to his dessert.

Her salad was prepared and her fish dinner was five minutes away from being done when he came in the door. He carried two bags full of food in his arms, which he set down on the counter.

He gave her a kiss, gave her a hug, said "I'll be with you in a minute, honey," then went to the bedroom to change his clothes.

It took all of her self-control not to peek in the bags. She was better off not knowing what he had until she had started to eat her own dinner. But just once, couldn't he eat fish? Or a broiled chicken breast? Or a Caesar salad? Did he always have to eat things that were visually gorgeous and smelled divine and were so full of calories they couldn't even be counted?

It was wearing her down. Everything else about their marriage was perfect, but the discrepancies in their eating patterns were getting harder and harder to live with. And it wasn't a small thing, either. Not when a good portion of their time together was spent eating. Well, a good portion of hers—almost *all* of his.

She had her dinner on the table and was already eating her salad when he came back in wearing jeans and a T-shirt. "Won my case today," he told her.

"Did you? That's great!" She couldn't remember what the case was about, though, and thought it was too late now to ask.

"I demolished the DA's case."

A criminal case, then. "Good for you!"

"What kind of day did you have?"

She swallowed a less-than-filling piece of lettuce and answered him. "Tense."

"Yeah? Bad day? Someone jump bail on you?" He reached into one of the bags and started pulling out cartons of Chinese food.

"No one jumped bail. I just get a little tense when it comes time for you to read one of my chapters."

The table was now literally covered with food cartons, and he went to get himself a beer.

"Hey," he said. "We've come a long way on this book. I thought you were past that fear of criticism you had at the beginning."

"I don't worry about your criticizing my writing. It's the content that worries me."

He sat down, consumed several spare ribs in the blink of an eye, then wiped off his hands as he said, "I see you got some sex in."

"I thought it needed a little."

"It was very tastefully done." On top of a thick bed of fried rice, he was dumping the contents of several containers. It created a mound that could pass for a mountain.

"It turned out I couldn't do it, either. I meant to write a great detailed sex scene, but it was embarrassing."

"And nobody's business but our own. I see you sneaked 'manhood' in there."

"That was just for you, just to be funny. I'll take it out."

"Don't, I liked it. It was cute."

"A little too cute."

"Listen, if they don't like it, they can take it out."

He continued eating, then paused for a moment. "You want some of this?" he asked her, waving one arm over the Chinese food.

"No thanks."

"I always heard Chinese food wasn't fattening."

"What you always heard was that it wasn't filling. It's plenty fattening. And worse."

He chuckled. "Worse? I thought in your book, fattening was as bad as you could get."

"It also has MSG in it, which isn't good for you."

"Hell, nothing that tastes any good is good for you."

He had a point. Her salad was varied and crisp; her fish and vegetable dinner was adequate; but none of it really tasted *good*. Nothing had really tasted good in a very long time.

He had demolished most of the food on the table before he said, "I'm getting a little annoyed by your attitude."

"My attitude?"

"Every chance you get in that book you sound off about my eating habits. You make me sound like a pig."

This coming from a man who had just consumed enough to feed a starving Chinese family of four for six months?

"I go to all the trouble to fix you a great Christmas breakfast—which you ate, as I recall—and then you go on and on about it as though I'm the one who eats abnormally. If I didn't know you'd once been fat, I'd say you had a bad case of anorexia."

The urge to dump the contents of the table into his lap came over her. To restrain herself, she carried her plate over to the sink.

"I'm not finished," he said.

"I'm listening."

"You take half the pleasure out of life. We go to a ball game and you refuse to eat a hot dog. We drive past a fast-food place and you refuse to go in. You never even want to go out to eat. And when I bring home something I think might really please you, you turn your nose up at it. What I'm trying to say is, you've become a fanatic. You're so afraid of being fat again, you're afraid to eat like a normal person. I mean hell, do you think one lousy pound is going to ruin you for life?"

She turned around to confront him. "I'm not a normal person. I was as addicted to food as some people are to alcohol."

"I don't believe that. You just think you are. And there's a big difference between indulging in food once in a while and indulging in liquor."

"What's the big difference?" she asked him.

"For one thing, food doesn't make you sloppy drunk. The cops won't ticket you for driving under the influence of ice cream. You won't wake up with a hangover."

"No, you'll just wake up fat."

"With all the running you do, I bet you couldn't gain a pound if you tried."

"Are you finished with those cartons?"

"Just sit down a minute, will you?"

"I'll just start cleaning up."

"Could we finish this discussion, please?"

She saw the serious look in his eyes, heard the note of exasperation in his voice. She sat back down at the table, trying to keep her eyes off the remains of his food.

He got up and walked over to the counter and pulled a bakery box out of the other bag. He carried it back to the table and shoved aside a few cartons to make room for it.

"Do you know what this is?" he asked her.

"No."

"It's a cinnamon raisin coffee cake."

She swallowed.

"The kind you thought of strangling me for."

"That was only a figure of speech."

"It didn't strike me that way. It sounded a lot more serious than that. How do you think it feels to eat all your meals with someone who feels like killing you for some of your food?"

"I wasn't serious."

"You *were* serious. I can feel the hatred coming at me from your side of the table every time we eat."

"You know I love you."

"Yeah, sure, some of the time. Not when we eat, though."

He broke the string on the box and opened the lid. The scent of cinnamon wafted over to her side of the table and she thought she'd die of longing.

"Look at you," he said. "I wish you could see yourself in a mirror." He lifted out the coffee cake and held it up. "You're looking at this coffee cake with more lust than you've ever looked at me."

"You're jealous of a coffee cake?"

He gave her a reproving look before setting the cake back down. This time it was out of the box, though, where she could clearly see it.

"I'm going to cut you a piece of this," he said.

"Please, no."

"Just a small piece. Just enough so that you can satisfy that craving of yours, but not enough to send you to the bathroom to throw it up."

"I never did that," she said. "I know people who do, but I never did. I lost my weight the healthy way."

"All right. Not enough to put on any weight, okay?"

"I can't eat a small piece."

"Yes, you can."

"I don't mean that physically I can't eat it. I mean that I don't think I'd be able to stop at one small piece."

He looked at her in curiosity. "Why not?"

"You're asking *me* why not? Why can't you stop with one potato chip? Or one piece of candy? Or one dish of ice cream?"

"That's not the same. I just have a big appetite."

"Well, most of my life I had a big appetite, too."

"But now you don't. Now you're satisfied with small portions. So you'll be satisfied with a small portion of this, too. And after you've eaten it you won't begrudge me having some dessert. You won't stare at me with loathing while I have it."

"I can leave the room while you have dessert."

He ignored her offer and got up for a plate and a knife. When he came back to the table, he slowly cut a very small portion of the cake and placed it on the plate. Then he set it down in front of her.

She could've buried her face in that piece of coffee cake it smelled so good. Despite the fact she had just finished her quota of food for the day, she felt herself salivating. She was as bad as an animal. She *was* an animal!

"Do you need a fork or can you pick it up and eat it?"

Maybe she could. Maybe she could eat that piece of coffee cake and feel better for it. Maybe it was actually possible for her to eat like a human being again.

She saw him go back to the counter and lift another box out of the bakery bag and transfer it to the refrigerator. "What's in that?" she asked him.

"Seven-layer cake."

She relaxed a little. She liked seven-layer cake, but it wasn't one of her fantasies. She'd take cinnamon raisin coffee cake over it any day.

He handed her a clean fork. "Go on, dig in."

"Aren't you having anything?"

He pulled a third box out of the bag. "I'm just going to have a couple of cupcakes. I'm pretty full."

He loaded four chocolate cupcakes with white icing onto a plate and brought them over to the table. As he slid the wrapping off the first one, she made a tentative move with her fork toward the coffee cake.

It was soft. Freshly baked. She could taste it before it even got to her mouth. And when it did get there, it practically melted in it. She could taste sugar and cinnamon and thick, fresh dough. She could count multitudes of calories headed straight for her stomach.

She looked up and caught him smiling at her. "See?" he asked. "Isn't that good?"

But she was already taking her second bite. She wanted to put down the fork and just pick it up and shove it in her mouth, but she restrained herself. Now she knew why she was able to eat slowly these days. It was because nothing tasted this good. When it tasted this good, you had to eat it quickly. You had to devour it whole!

He still had a whole cupcake to go by the time she finished. But she wasn't looking at the cupcake. She was looking at the remainder of the coffee cake.

"See?" he asked. "It didn't kill you, did it? Run in and weigh yourself if you're worried about it."

"Who's going to eat the rest?"

He smiled at her. "Don't worry about it. You can have another little piece for breakfast, and I'll have the rest."

"I want another piece."

"No one's stopping you. Help yourself." He even handed her the knife.

She put her brain on hold, so she wouldn't know what she was doing, and then she cut herself another piece of the coffee cake. Larger this time.

"You want a beer with that?"

She shook her head. Beer didn't go with coffee cake. What she wanted with it was hot chocolate with whipped cream. She felt deprived that there wasn't any in the house.

She got hold of herself after the second piece and forced herself to get up from the table. They cleaned up the kitchen together, then went into the living room to watch the baseball game.

During the first commercial, she started to get up and he said, "Get me a beer while you're up, okay? And maybe some of those Oreos?"

She stopped by the kitchen long enough to get the box of coffee cake, then headed for the bathroom. With the door locked, she consumed the rest of it in silence. She ate it quickly, hardly chewing it, but she enjoyed every morsel.

When she got back to the living room, he said, "What took you so long?"

"I went to the bathroom."

She thought she could breathe easy now. The coffee cake was gone. She couldn't be tempted to have any more because there wasn't any more. She was safe for the moment.

Except that then she remembered the seven-layer cake. All that soft yellow cake; all those layers of icing. All that goodness and sweetness sitting in the bakery box in the refrigerator.

"You want another beer?" she asked him.

"I'll take some of those fortune cookies."

She headed once again for the kitchen.

By the time the game was over, so was the cake. And the Mallomars. And several of his Mars bars. And the last time she went into the kitchen, the time she found a bag of marshmallows in the cupboard and was stuffing them into her mouth, he caught her.

"What're you doing?" he asked her.

"Nothing."

He opened the refrigerator door and looked inside. "Where's the seven-layer cake?"

"I don't know."

He gave her a disbelieving look and walked over to the trash can.

She panicked. "Don't open that!"

He lifted the lid and looked inside. "My God, did you eat all that?"

"You eat that much every night."

"You really can't control yourself, can you?"

"When have you ever controlled yourself?" she shouted at him.

"Hey, relax—I'm not going to punish you."

She found herself shaking. There wasn't anything more to eat, and if there was, he wouldn't let her have it. They were going to fight over who got the food.

"Honey, are you all right?"

"No, I'm not all right," she said, tears of frustration springing to her eyes. "I'm a foodaholic and I can't stand living with you!"

"Look, I made a mistake, I admit it. I had no idea you'd pig out like that."

"You wanted me to. You want me to be just like you!"

"I'd like us to be more compatible when it comes to food, yes."

"Well, we're not. You're sick! You shove food in your mouth like you're starving to death! I can't take it anymore!"

"I'm not the one who's sick," he said softly.

She threw the bag of marshmallows at him and ran out of the room.

She was packing when he came into the bedroom. "What do you think you're doing?" he asked her.

"I can't live with you," she said. "I've tried and I can't do it."

"Honey, you're making too big a deal out of this."

"Just pretend I'm roaring drunk, okay? Just leave me alone!"

"I can't belive you're acting like this."

"Oh, yes, just stand there being calm and reasonable. I should've known that first night I went out with you that it was no good. I did know it! And I was right. Your eating habits disgust me and I don't want to be around you anymore."

His face crumpled as though she had hit him. "I'm sorry I disgust you."

When she didn't say anything, he walked out of the room. The next thing she heard was him opening the refrigerator, then the sound of a tab being pulled off a can of beer.

Five minutes later she walked out of the house.

Chapter Eight

A restless Bobby was stalking around Tom's office, pausing now and then to turn on one of the neon lights and watch it flash. Tom had given him his "sincere" speech, his "I always do my best for my client" speech, but he wasn't sure Bobby had bought it. That was understandable, of course.

Bobby paused in front of one of Tom's favorites, the one with the moose head that lit up in four colors, and stood there eye to eye with the moose. "I don't know whether I trust you," he said, and since his back was to Tom it was almost as though the moose was speaking to him.

Tom stared that moose in the face. It was now past the time for being sincere. It was bluffing time. "I think what you ought to do, Bobby, is find yourself a new lawyer. If you have any doubts at all about my having your best interests at heart, then you owe it to yourself to find someone who does."

He thought he knew his client. Bobby wasn't the kind of person who shopped around for lawyers. Bobby was the type to open a phone book and pick out the first name he spotted. He was sure that Bobby believed that the case would be won or lost on his personal charm alone, and nothing a lawyer did or didn't do was going to change the verdict.

Bobby pulled the cord on the moose light and was suddenly blinded by four-color flashing. He turned back to Tom, squinting. "You and that lady from the DA's office, you looked pretty chummy at the club that night."

"We went to law school together."

"You guys friends?"

"More like friendly adversaries."

Bobby drifted over to another part of the room and stood beneath Tom's laminated diplomas from college and law school. He was nodding his head as though reading some message there, although Tom somehow doubted that Bobby understood Latin. When he turned around, he said, "I never got past high school." He made it sound as though there were something suspect about someone who did.

"I never would've gone to law school if I could've made it as a stand-up comic," said Tom.

Bobby took a seat in one of the chairs, then slid down so his head was resting on the back. His mouth curved into something resembling a smirk. "Show me."

"What?"

"Let's see one of your routines."

Tom wasn't sure whether he was joking, was really taking an interest in his comic ability, or whether he was hoping Tom would be so bad he could fire him on the spot for incompetence. In any case, Tom wasn't taking any chances. "I don't do it anymore," said Tom.

"Out of practice?"

"I'm a better lawyer than a comic."

Bobby seemed satisfied with the answer. "Okay, Cunningham, I guess I'll go with you. Now that you got it straight that you're not supposed to be socializing with the prosecution witnesses."

Tom would much rather be socializing with one particular prosecution witness, but since she wasn't eager to socialize with him... "If you're sure about that, Bobby, then I think we ought to get down to business."

"Hey, no hard feelings," said Bobby. "Listen, I don't blame you. Those Benson girls, they're something else, huh?"

Was Tom hearing right? Bobby was lumping Holly and Tiffany into the same category?

"And their mom! Is she a great cook, or what?"

Tom smiled at the memory. "The greatest."

Bobby gave him an expansive smile. "So how's the case coming?"

"I need to ask you a few questions."

"Shoot."

"Where'd you get the gun?"

"Oh, that. I got it from my mom."

"The gun belongs to your mother?"

"It's not exactly legal—at least not in New York. My mom picked it up last time she was down in Florida."

"What for?"

"You don't need a reason down there. You can just walk in anywhere and get a gun, no questions asked. My aunt drove her down, and she got one, too."

"But why did she want a gun?"

"Why not? Down there it's like buying a screwdriver or a hammer, you know? It's just something to have around the house."

"She bought it for protection?"

"Oh, yeah—Mom's big on protection. She got a burglar alarm system, about a trillion locks on all the doors, bars over all the windows and a pit bull in the backyard. Harvey. None of us go near him."

Tom made a mental note to stay away from the vicinity of Bobby's house. "So what were you doing with the gun?"

"I had it in mind to kidnap Holly."

"*Kidnap?* Your intention was to kidnap her?"

"Hey, we're not talking *real* kidnapping here. I mean I wasn't taking her across no state lines or nothin'."

"Where were you going to take her?"

"You know that motel on Ocean Drive? The one with the separate little cabins?"

Tom nodded. When he was in high school it was the one the boys all kidded about taking the girls to. Only the girls were wise to them and wouldn't go.

"I figured I'd take her there. The thing is, she wouldn't talk to me. I was just going to force her to talk to me, that's all."

A picture began to form in Tom's mind of Holly being taken by gunpoint to a motel room and forced to listen to Bobby. And, after she listened, would they have made love? Did she still have some feelings for this idiot? And yet he'd bet that half the women in the audience the other night would've gone to that motel with him.

"Okay," said Bobby, taking his silence for disapproval. "So it was the wrong way to go about it. I was desperate. My mother keeps harping on me day and night, 'Why don't you move out of the house?' 'Why can't you get your wife back?' 'What kind of a man are you that you couldn't make Holly happy?' She's wearin' me down, you know?"

"You must have had other women since your divorce," said Tom. "It looked to me like all the ladies went for you."

"Yeah, it looks that way. But I told you—it's Elvis they want. Since he's dead, I'm the only way they can have him, you know what I mean? The thing is, every woman I've gone with except Holly won't let me stop being Elvis for a minute. It gets tiring. It even gives me a sore throat talking like that all the time. When I'm just being myself, they lose interest. Not too many women are interested in a bus mechanic for the Metropolitan Transit Authority."

"All right. So you were going to take Holly—at gun-point—to a motel and talk to her. You were trying to get her to go back to you, right?"

"Right."

"What if she had said no? What then?"

"I figured I could talk her into it."

"But if you hadn't succeeded, what would you have done?"

"I guess I didn't think it out that much. I just figured, if I could get her alone, I could sweet-talk her into it."

"You weren't going to use the gun?"

"Yeah, I told you. To get her to go there with me."

"I mean afterward."

"You mean was I going to *shoot* her? What're ya, crazy?"

"The jury is going to wonder about that gun."

"I didn't even know it was loaded until I blew a hole in the ceiling."

"Hey, calm down. I just want to prepare you for some of the questions you're going to be asked on the stand."

"Holly knows I wouldn't shoot her. I never laid a hand on that woman in my life. On any woman."

"So what changed your mind when you got to the Weight Watchers meeting? Why didn't you take her to the motel?"

"Ah, things got all screwed up. Just when I thought I was going to take her out of there, the police show up. It's all of a sudden a hostage situation, can you believe it?"

"So why didn't you give yourself up at that point?"

"Because I had a better idea. From the moment I walked in, those people were poking their noses in our business. They got me mad, taking Holly's side the way they did. So I figured maybe if I could convince *them*, maybe Holly'd be convinced, too."

"So you had yourself a mock trial in there."

"Yeah. What a mistake. Those Weight Watchers people are brutal, you know that? There wasn't one person who took my side. I swear, you'd think Holly was some saint the way they carried on."

Tom thought of telling the jury about this poor, desperate man, still in love with his wife who spurned all his attempts at reconciliation, finally driven to invade a Weight Watchers meeting intending to carry her off to a motel. Was it romantic or blatant nonsense?

He thought it was blatant nonsense, but you could never be sure how a jury would react.

IT HAD BEEN the best Christmas in memory, but it was shaping up to be a lousy New Year's Eve. Too bad, too, because it could have been the best ever.

Every other woman he had ever dated during the holidays had wanted to dress up on New Year's Eve and go dancing. In anticipation of going out with Holly New Year's Eve, Tom had purchased two tickets to the Knicks game. Afterward he had intended taking her to the Improv to see the new comedians try out their acts. They could eat there, get a few drinks and be guaranteed some laughs.

It was really stupid. They were in love, weren't they? They had said they were. He knew for sure *he* was. And they were going to spend New Year's Eve apart? Just so he could try a criminal case? It didn't make sense. It was a hell of a way to start off such a great romance.

New Year's Eve turned out to be a real bummer. He had called up all his old buddies, trying to find someone who might want to go to the game with him. In the old days, tickets to a Knicks game would have caused most of them to break any date they might have. Now, most of them he could even locate were either married or unwilling to change their plans. They all said things like, "Let's get together sometime," or "Let's catch a game after the first of the year," but that wasn't what he wanted to hear.

He called a couple of comedian friends of his, guys he had done the comedy circuit with, but one's phone number was disconnected and the other one's mother told him that Jim was now on the West Coast and getting TV work. So Jim had made it and all Tom was doing was defending a fake terrorist.

He ended up not even using the tickets and not being able to find anyone who'd take them off his hands. He got in a supply of beer and stuff to snack on and stayed home to watch the game by himself.

Halfway into the game he was already on his way to becoming roaring drunk. So drunk he dialed Holly's number, determined to talk to her, to wish her a happy New Year if nothing else, but she didn't answer the phone. It became paranoia time. Was she out with someone else? Had she gone to some party where at this moment men were surrounding her, begging her for her phone number? Had she gone to the Knicks game and was right now sitting in the Garden having a great time while he was home getting drunk alone?

This kind of thing precipitated him getting all the way smashed, but by the time the game ended he had already sobered up and was suffering from a hangover. And it wasn't even midnight yet.

What he needed to do was get out of the house. Maybe go somewhere and get another drink, which would be just the ticket to take care of his hangover. And tomorrow he'd take it easy on the beer during the bowl games.

Since it was New Year's Eve, he got into a sport jacket and slacks, then drove to the Skylark Lounge. It was the kind of place that was going to be so crowded no one would even notice he was alone. He could just blend into the crowd, catch Bobby's act, and maybe stop feeling sorry for himself.

There was a cover charge, which he hadn't anticipated. He paid the forty dollars, fought his way to the bar, and had a beer in his hand by the time Bobby came out for the midnight show. The place was packed. It was rather like riding the subway at rush hour the way the bodies were so thick that every time he lifted his beer to take a drink, he had to say "excuse me" to the several people he poked with his elbow.

Bobby was in lime-green satin tonight, his pompadour stiff and glistening, his gyrations becoming frenzied by the end of his first song. The women were going crazy, screaming every time his hips took off in a different direction, which was constantly. As had happened on his previous visit to the Skylark, women kept running up to the stage to be kissed by the fake Elvis until it was almost a stampede. He wondered whether Bobby ever worried about picking up social diseases that way. Bobby didn't look as though he worried about anything. Bobby looked like he was eating it up.

Tom started to get angry. Here was Bobby, all the women after him, packing them in because of his foolhardy attempt at terrorism. He was cashing in on that attempt, while he and Holly were kept apart, and all because of that idiot on the stage in his garish satin suit. It wasn't fair. To hell with Bobby. To hell with his first criminal case. He'd rather have Holly any day of the week than defend the biggest criminal in the country, and that Bobby wasn't.

He was going to leave the club and drive by her trailer right now. If she was home, great. If she wasn't, he'd wait for her. He didn't believe for a moment she'd be out with someone else. She might even be over at her mom's house, in which case he'd drive by there, too. He'd be damned if he was going to see the new year in with a bar full of strangers. If you weren't with the one you loved on New Year's Eve, what was the point of even celebrating?

Leaving the club turned out to be easier said than done. Tom kept excusing himself as he shoved his way through the crowd, but as soon as he had gotten a few feet nearer to the entrance, more people would come through the door and propel him back. He had a feeling they were breaking a few fire laws by letting so many people into the club, but at forty dollars a shot, they probably were willing to risk it.

Through much devious maneuvering, he finally found himself near the entrance. A scream went up and he turned for one last look at Bobby. He appeared to have stepped off the stage and was wending his way through the tables, microphone in hand, singing "Love Me Tender." The woman at the tables were practically passing out from excitement.

Bobby appeared to be heading for one particular table, and Tom looked over in that direction. He had to take a second look before he believed what he was seeing.

Holly was seated at the table with her sister, Tiffany. Both of them were smiling in anticipation of Bobby's imminent arrival.

Tom went home and got drunk.

Interlude

She received the envelope in the mail on Monday and waited until she got home to read the chapter.

The trailer didn't seem like home anymore. The plants had all been transferred to their house, where she hoped he was watering them. Without the plants it had no charm or warmth. It was just a mostly empty trailer that seemed to attract dust.

She changed into her running shorts and a T-shirt and set off in the direction of the beach. She knew she was purposely prolonging the time when she'd read the chapter; she wasn't even sure she wanted to read it. She missed him so much that reading it wasn't going to be easy.

It wasn't as though she didn't need to run. She desperately needed to run. The binge that had begun during their last fight had escalated, not brought to a halt until a few days later.

On Sunday, the day after she had walked out, she had gone to the supermarket and bought everything she ever wanted to eat. She bought two of most things. She had filled her refrigerator and cupboards with all the goodies she had felt deprived of, and then had methodically eaten it all. She'd eaten cookies and candy and donuts and cakes and pies with whipped cream piled on top. She ate peanut butter and jelly sandwiches on thick, crusty French bread and pounds of lasagna and fashioned her own banana splits. She ate chocolate-covered pretzels washed down with soft drinks and an entire giant-sized box of Frosted Flakes.

She was out of control and knew it. And yet she also knew that she wasn't eating anything he couldn't eat and get away with, and the knowledge of that made her angry. And the angrier she got, the more she ate, not caring that it was the worst kind of self-destruction.

When she had finally consumed everything in the house, which took a few days, she got on the scale and weighed herself. The weight gain was only a couple of pounds, but she knew that was deceptive. Weight gains were cumulative and she'd see the total damage in several days. In the meantime, she felt guilty and sick to her stomach and generally miserable.

For the next two days she starved herself. She ate nothing and drank gallons of water, hoping against hope that she could wash out all the damage before it turned to fat. And then she began to run. She ran miles in the morning and miles at night, hoping to exhaust herself so that she'd be able to sleep.

She wasn't sleeping well at all, though. She missed him. She missed the talking and joking around in bed. She missed his arms around her when she fell asleep. She missed waking up to his lips on hers. She missed everything about him except his eating habits. And yet they were such that they overshadowed everything else.

Once in a while she told herself the hell with it. She'd go back to him, she'd eat the way he did, and she'd gradually put all her weight back on. But she'd still have him and she thought he'd still love her. The only problem was, she wouldn't love herself. She'd hate her body and gradually she'd hate herself for allowing it to happen.

She looked down at her slim, muscular legs as she ran and knew what it would do to her to be seeing again those fat appendages that couldn't even run a block. If she could even *see* her legs over her stomach.

Her binge had been over by the time she led her Weight Watchers session. She decided binges would be her topic that night, and she found herself confessing her own binge to the group. Some of them looked at her in amazement as though they thought she was above such things, but the others were sympathetic.

When she asked for advice, some of it was surprising. Arnold said he thought she had made a mistake in marrying a man who never gained an ounce and ate all the time. He said that personally he'd go crazy living with someone like that. Sylvia suggested that they go to a marriage counselor, adding that she and her husband went to one frequently. Phyllis had the most novel suggestion. She said that it might be a good idea if they fixed up one room of the house as his eating room, where he could go when he needed to eat and she wouldn't have to watch him.

The thing was, it was hardly fair to make him go to a special room to eat in his own house. And since he ate almost constantly, that meant she'd rarely see him.

Of course at the moment she wasn't seeing him at all.

At least she had no more desire to binge. She was back to eating healthily and was feeling much better for it. And if she kept running and running and running, maybe the binge wouldn't result in any real damage.

She was soaked with sweat when she got back to the trailer and showered before sitting down with the chapter. She took a folding chair outside to get some sun while she read it, and then began.

The first thing she noticed was that it was short. That was okay, though; she hadn't really expected him to even write it that week. She thought her leaving would mean the end of the book.

When she got to the part about him staying home alone on New Year's Eve, she was saddened. It hadn't been so great spending the night with her sister, but it had to be better than spending it alone. What a shame that they missed out on a Knicks game just because of Bobby. It really wasn't worth it.

When she went back and read it again, she noticed something she should have noticed the first time. He appeared to have done a lot of drinking and didn't think twice about it.

Now that she thought about it, it was rare not to see a can of beer in his hand. Bobby had always been able to put them away, but even Bobby had never drunk that much. Was it possible that he had a drinking problem?

The more she thought about it the more she worried. Was always having a beer in hand a sign of alcoholism? Granted, he didn't drink first thing in the morning, and as far as she knew he didn't drink on the job, but other than that he was just about always drinking. This could be a lot more serious than his eating habits.

Maybe he should look into joining AA. And maybe, if he did join AA, he would be more understanding of what she went through with food.

She went back inside to call him, glad of the excuse. She had been waiting for him to be the one to call first, but he had made the first move by sending her the chapter and now it was up to her.

He picked up the phone on the second ring and she could hear the sound of the TV in the background.

"Hello?"

"Hi," she said. "It's me."

"Did you get the chapter?"

"That's why I'm calling."

"Oh." He sounded disappointed.

"How're you doing?"

"Okay. What about you?"

"Okay. Now." Now that she had stopped her binge.

"So, was it okay? I didn't feel much like writing it, which probably showed."

"It was short, but I guess that's all right. I figure you can make the trial chapter longer."

"I have to write that, huh?"

"Definitely. Everyone's going to want to know what happened to Bobby."

"I figured they'd want to know what happened to us."

"Oh, of course. That too. It's going to have to be a happy ending, even if—"

"Yeah, that's what I thought."

She said, "There's one thing I noticed in that part about New Year's Eve."

"I didn't really think you were there because you still liked Bobby."

"I wasn't. Tiffany dragged me there."

"It's just that there you were, out having a good time, and I was really feeling sorry for myself."

"I wasn't having a good time."

"You looked like you were."

"Well, I was feeling pretty good, being in love and all, even if we couldn't be together."

"So what part didn't you like?"

She said, "It wasn't that I didn't like it—I like the way you write."

"Then what was it?"

She hesitated for a moment. "Well, it seemed like you were doing a lot of drinking that night."

"I was. Can't you mention drinking in these books?"

"Sure. It's just that, drunk two times in one night?"

"That's not okay?"

"I'm not talking about the book. I'm talking about you. It occurred to me that you might have a . . . a drinking problem."

There was a long silence. "Did I hear you correctly?" His voice had lost some of its warmth.

"You do drink a lot."

"Beer. All I ever drink is beer. It's not like I'm chugging down whiskey."

"It's still alcohol," she said.

"Wait a minute. Let me get this straight. Are you accusing me of being an alcoholic?"

"I'm not accusing you of anything. I'm just pointing out that there may be a problem you're not even aware of."

"What is this?" he asked. "You think just because you have some kind of a problem, everyone does? Is that it?"

"Why are you getting so defensive?"

"Because I'm trying to defend myself, that's why. I think it's perfectly normal to get defensive when someone accuses you of being an alcoholic."

"Obviously I shouldn't have brought it up. It seems to be a touchy subject."

She heard the phone crash down and a moment later the sound of the TV was silenced. When he came back to the phone he said, "You're wrong. It's not a touchy subject because it's not a subject that's ever been brought up before. By anyone."

"Well, maybe no one's been with you as much as I have."

"I don't believe this," he said. "I watch you go into some bizarre eating binge, then you walk out of here and the next thing I know you're as good as saying I'm a drunk."

"How many beers have you had so far this evening?"

"None of your damn business. I'm not drunk, am I?"

"You certainly lost your temper pretty quickly."

"Not because of any beer I might've consumed."

"Look, I'm sorry I mentioned it."

"Not as sorry as I am."

"But I don't think it would hurt you to go to an AA meeting. Sometimes people have drinking problems and aren't even aware of it."

There was another silence. "You're not going to let go of this, are you? Look, hold on a minute while I get another beer."

She waited, wondering if she was the cause of his drinking. Maybe he started drinking so much when he met her. Maybe there was something about her that made him want to drink.

When he came back to the phone, he said, "You're driving me to drink."

"I can understand that. You drove me to eat."

"I was only kidding."

"Well, look, I guess I shouldn't have mentioned it."

"You shouldn't have even *thought* it."

"I was worried about you."

"You don't have to worry about me. Worry about yourself—you're the one with the problem."

"Thanks a lot."

"You're welcome."

She slammed down the phone and burst into tears.

Chapter Nine

The telephone call came late at night and the voice was muffled. It woke Holly up and for a moment she thought it was going to be an obscene phone call. The problem with that was, she was half-asleep and she couldn't think of anything insulting enough to say.

Then she heard, "Are you the person interested in one of my collages?"

Holly came wide awake. "Is this Mr. Sykol?"

"Uh, yes. They told me at the gallery you wanted to talk to me."

"Did they tell you I wanted to talk to you in the middle of the night?"

"Sorry. Do you want me to call back tomorrow?"

Holly turned on the lamp and sat up in bed. "No, that's all right. I'm up now. Listen, I really love those collages of yours. I've never seen anything like them."

"I'm pretty sure there isn't anything like them, unless someone's ripping them off already."

"They're absolutely unique," said Holly, knowing that artists needed their egos soothed. "I would just love to own one."

"Well, they're for sale."

"Yes," said Holly, wondering if she should try to get him down on the price for form's sake. If she was too easy a sale, he might get suspicious. "The woman at the gallery mentioned that you were asking a thousand for them. That's a little steep for me."

"How high would you be willing to go?"

"What's your lowest price?"

"Make me an offer."

So the ball was back to her. Not that it mattered what she offered him since she wasn't going to buy it anyway. "How about five hundred?"

"I could really use seven-fifty."

Holly audibly sighed.

"How about six-fifty?" he asked, no doubt afraid that she had fallen back asleep.

"All right," said Holly. "It's a little more than I can afford right after the holidays, but I know it's worth it."

"You're getting a bargain."

"Well, I'm excited. I can't wait to get it."

"You can pick it up anytime. There's just one problem, I only take cash."

"Cash?"

Now she could hear him sigh. "You wouldn't believe all the phony checks the gallery has taken in. You wouldn't think people would write bad checks for art, but they do."

"All right, I can just as easily pay you cash."

"Great. Only you don't pay me—just pay whoever's in the gallery. I'll tell them to expect you."

"Oh, no—I was so looking forward to meeting you. I've met every artist I've bought work from. I think it makes it much more personal, don't you?"

"I'm afraid that's not convenient for me at the moment."

"Oh, please, it would mean so much."

"Maybe another time."

Holly let the silence stretch a little. "Well, in that case, I think I'll wait until that time to purchase it. I mean, what if you turned out to be another Van Gogh or something and I hadn't gotten to meet you? I'd be devastated, Mr. Sykol."

A pause. "Could you meet me at the gallery at night?"

"I don't see why not."

"I mean late at night. Like this time."

"At two-thirty in the morning?"

"Would that be possible?"

"I guess so," said Holly. "Sure, why not? I know how eccentric you artists are."

"Would tomorrow night be okay?"

Holly pretended to think about it for a moment, then said, "Tomorrow night's okay with me. How's that neighborhood at night?"

"Quiet and uneventful."

"Fine. I'll see you then, Mr. Sykol. And I really appreciate your getting in touch with me." By then, though, he had already hung up.

"YOU'RE ASKING FOR a stakeout?" Sgt. Bono looked less than pleased with the request.

"He skipped, didn't he? Don't you have a warrant out on him?"

"Holly, I'd like to help you out, but you know how short-staffed we are with all the cuts in the department."

"You sure had enough men out there to surround my ex, Bono. You had everything but the National Guard."

"That was different. That was a hostage situation."

"Baloney," said Holly. "That was my ex showing off, that's all, and on account of it he's getting famous."

Bono grinned at her. "Yeah, I caught his act the other night. He's okay, you know? Really looked like Elvis."

"I help you out, I find a wanted criminal for you—"

"You just don't want to lose the bail money."

"You're damn right I don't," said Holly. "We're talking about nine thousand dollars."

"You coulda given me a little notice."

"He called me in the middle of the night! Come on, you expecting a big crime spree in Rocky Inlet at two-thirty in the morning?"

"You never know."

"I do all the work for you and this is the thanks I get. I guess I'm going to have to go in and talk to Lieutenant Keely."

"Leave Keely out of this."

"You're giving me no choice," said Holly, putting on an innocent look.

"We're even getting coerced by the bail bondsmen now, I don't believe it."

"Bail bondsperson, Bono."

"Whatever. Okay, Holly, I'll see what I can do for you."

"I want to know now, Bono. I'm not trotting over there at two-thirty in the morning to meet some felon who thinks I'm going to hand over six hundred and fifty dollars in cash and then get stuck alone with him."

"Will the gallery cooperate? Can we get a man in there?"

"I doubt it. I think those artists would stick together. It's a cooperative they have over there."

"So what do my men do, jump out of the bushes?"

"Do what they do on TV, Bono—have them parked in a van on the street with the name of a business on the side of it."

"That's for big drug stakeouts, Holly. We're talking peanuts here."

"Fine. Suit yourself. Have them jump out of the bushes."

"Let me think about it. I'll call you later and let you know how we're going to set it up."

"Surprise me," said Holly.

SHE HAD A WEIGHT WATCHERS meeting that night and it was just as well as she would have been too nervous to sit around the house and wait until it was time to meet Sykol. Ideally, she would have spent the time with Tom. On the other hand, Tom might've objected to her setting up Sykol to begin with. He might also be the worrying kind.

It was the first meeting since the holidays and Holly noticed a few strange faces. They usually picked up new members after holidays where people overindulged and then felt guilty. She had overindulged herself. She weighed herself at the front desk and found she had gained half a pound. She was sure that that memorable Christmas breakfast had been responsible, but since it was also in lieu of a memorable night, she didn't regret it. She'd just run an extra mile or two the next few days and that ought to take it off.

Holly had the new members introduce themselves, and then she asked, "How did it go? Did any of you lose weight over the holidays?"

One hand shot up. When Holly said, "Good for you, Phyllis," Sylvia spoke up, saying, "She wasn't good—she had the flu. I should get so lucky."

"How many of you maintained?" Holly asked them, and about half the hands went up.

"So you gained a little," said Holly. "It's to be expected over the holidays. Just think of it this way— how much more would you have gained if you weren't a member of Weight Watchers?"

"Tons more," said Sylvia, and there were nods of agreement all around.

"I gained half a pound," admitted Holly. "And you know what I'm going to do about it?"

"Get back on program," said Arnold, which was what she usually advised them to do.

"That, too," said Holly, "but I'm also going to run a few more miles a week. How about the rest of you? Are you exercising?"

There were a lot of groans and a lot of averted eyes. Then one of the younger members spoke up. "I work out at my health club every day."

There were more groans, and she thought she could hear Sylvia mutter, "Get her out of here!"

"You don't have to work out every day if that's not your thing," said Holly. "But all of you can walk. If nothing else, you can walk around the malls, and in this weather that's a good place to be."

"I walk around the malls all the time," said Sylvia.

"I don't mean shopping," said Holly. "It has to be a sustained walk in order to do any good. And that means not stopping to look in stores. But exercise isn't what I want to talk about tonight. What I want us to discuss is how supportive the people you live with are. Or aren't. Are any of you having any problems sticking to the program at home?"

Several hands went up and Holly called on Deborah, a recently married member.

"My husband likes to go out to eat at fast-food places and he gets mad when I won't go with him."

"Some of them have salad bars now," said Phyllis.

Deborah nodded. "But what I like best about Weight Watchers is that I don't have to just eat salads. And it makes me sick watching him shove all those burgers and fries in his mouth while I'm eating a not-very-exciting salad."

"Is he overweight?" asked Arnold.

"He's getting a gut, but he won't admit it."

"What about at home?" Holly asked her. "Are you having problems there?"

"Not so much, but that's because I do all the cooking. And I only cook what I can eat. But after dinner he snacks continuously until we go to bed."

"Does this bother you?" asked Holly.

"Sometimes," said Deborah. "When it does, I leave the room."

"What about the rest of you?" asked Holly. "Any advice for her?"

"Other than divorce?" asked Sylvia, which got a big laugh.

"I love him," said Deborah. "And I know he's proud of the weight I've lost. But he just doesn't see why he should change his eating habits for me."

Millicent, who was usually quiet, spoke up. "There's worse things than a husband who eats too much."

"There's got to be some give and take in marriage," said Phyllis. "My husband's doctor told him he had to give up smoking, and that was really hard for him. I don't think the time for me to give up smoking is when I'm trying to lose weight, so I still smoke, but not in the house and never around him."

"I think if I told John to give up eating around the house, he'd divorce me," said Deborah.

"Give it time," said Holly. "As you said, you're doing all the cooking. Once he gets used to eating the right way, he might decide he likes it. And he can always have larger portions."

"You can get used to anything in time," said Arnold. "I'm even getting used to getting up in the middle of the night to feed the baby."

That got a large round of applause from the women.

HOLLY WENT TO BED early and set the alarm for one-thirty, but she couldn't get to sleep. The meeting had disturbed her, particularly Deborah's problem.

She had an idea what Deborah was going through. Bobby had been a horror to live with once she began to lose weight. She didn't know whether it had to do with his power slipping away, the power a more attractive mate always held over a less attractive one, or whether he really had preferred her fat, as he always asserted. And yet she wasn't fat now and he had still made that stupid move to get her back.

Of course she never should have married Bobby in the first place. But what did she know at nineteen? Certainly nothing about boys. She had never dated in high school; instead she had spent Saturday nights with the other unpopular girls. Bobby was the first boy who ever asked her out. She had been dieting like crazy that summer, some stupid diet that she was lucky didn't damage her health. As she recalled, all she had eaten for weeks had been bananas and ice cream, and much as she liked both of them, there was only so much of either that she could eat.

She had met Bobby at her thinnest period, although she still had to buy her clothes at stores for large women. He had been good-looking and charming and sexy; he had an Elvis Presley act that thrilled her; and he was actually interested in *her*. At the time she couldn't believe her luck. They had been married two months later, and only then did she question whether Bobby wanted to be married to her or whether he just wanted to move out of his house but wanted someone to take his mother's place.

The marriage had been bad from the start, although she hadn't realized it at the time. Bobby, used to an abusive mother, was abusive to her in return. Not physically, but he sure had a mouth on him. He had never stopped goading her about being fat, while at the same time insisting on meals fit for stevedores, and because what he said to her made her unhappy, she ate when he wasn't around to make up for it, since from her family she had always equated food with love.

When, after eight years of mental abuse and having to live with the knowledge that her husband regularly cheated on her, she joined Weight Watchers and started to exercise and lose weight, Bobby got worse. He made fun of her new eating habits, he ridiculed her running, and he did everything in his power to get her back to the way she was before.

But there was no going back for Holly once she saw the pounds begin to disappear from her body. She felt better, she had more energy, and the beauty of it was she never felt she was starving.

Bobby, who enjoyed a good meal but wasn't much of a snacker, started to demand all kinds of goodies around the house. Every chance he got he ate sweets in front of her, even in bed. He made sure he left all her favorite things around to tempt her. He enlisted the support of her family, none of whom was thrilled by her steady weight loss. They made her feel as though she were deserting the family ship.

And yet she never really hated Bobby. He was a product of his home environment, just as she was of hers. Even if he had been supportive of her dieting, and even if the verbal abuse had stopped, the marriage would still have been doomed. Basically Bobby saw his wife as his possession, and that was something Holly resented from the start. She'd be no man's possession; she'd be her own person. Only with Bobby, that would never be possible.

She finally moved out and filed for divorce, and the past two years had been heaven for her. She had gone right from her parents' house to Bobby's and had never known the luxury of living alone. She had never had a refrigerator all to herself where forbidden foods didn't reside. She had never eaten meals alone and known the pleasure of getting up from the table when she was finished and not having to watch someone else keep eating. She had never known that running a business and supporting herself would give her such a feeling of self-worth. Once she knew it, she wasn't eager to give any of it up.

Tom was another matter altogether. Tom had all the good qualities that Bobby lacked, with some extras thrown in. And she truly loved Tom. They enjoyed the same things, shared the same sense of humor, and while his eating habits were deplorable, no one was perfect. And she could hardly suggest that he ate too much when he never seemed to gain an ounce.

Anyway, Tom was intelligent. She was sure that with no help from her, he'd come to realize that he still ate like a child. More and more men were learning to eat for health and to exercise for fitness; he just needed a good example.

And if he didn't change? Well, she would still love him. Love just wasn't that selective.

At one-thirty Holly got out of bed and dressed warmly. She had a cup of herbal tea to warm her up but not keep her up the rest of the night.

It was freezing out and it took her a while to get one of the cars started. She drove through quiet streets to the gallery and parked out in front. There were no lights on inside and when she knocked at the door, she didn't expect anyone to answer. It looked as though Sykol wasn't going to show and Bono was going to kill her if he didn't.

She knocked again and then looked around. She was sure there weren't any cops in the bushes because there weren't any bushes. There also wasn't a van parked anywhere on the street. There were cars, but none looked occupied.

Finally a light behind the door went on, and then the door opened and the woman she had talked to previously stood there. She was wearing a robe and slippers and her hair was mussed up.

"I'm supposed to meet Mr. Sykol here," said Holly.

"John's here. Come on in."

Holly looked over her shoulder before entering the building. There was still no sign of the cops and if they didn't show up, she was going to be forced into buying artwork she couldn't afford.

Holly stood in the entry hall while the woman disappeared into the dark gallery. A moment later lights went on and a voice said, "Come on in."

Holly entered and saw a skinny man in his forties with dark glasses and a beard. She had never seen Sykol, hadn't waited while the police had released him, so that now she wasn't certain this was the man. She belatedly realized she should have asked Bono for a description.

"Are you the artist?" Holly asked him.

The man nodded, moving to stand in the shadows.

The woman said, "Well, John, if you don't need me anymore, I'm going back to bed."

"Thanks, Susie."

Holly walked over to where Sykol's collages hung on the walls. She supposed she was going to have to pick one out. She was looking at them, one by one, when Sykol said, "That's my favorite."

Holly took a closer look at it. It had the requisite twenty dollar bills plastered all over it but the headlines on this one, rather than being cut from the financial pages, all had to do with rich people being killed for their money. One said, "Husband Kills Heiress," another read, "Daughter Blows Up Parents on Family Yacht," and a third proclaimed, "Millionaire Slain in Love Nest."

"I call it 'Greed,'" said Sykol.

Holly didn't even want to pretend to want that one. She moved past it to the next, glanced at it briefly, and said, "This is the one I'm interested in."

"That was a bad day for the stock market."

"So it would appear," said Holly, wondering when the cops were going to show up.

"Would you like me to wrap it up in brown paper for you?"

"That's not necessary. It'll be okay in the back seat of my car."

"If that's it, then...."

Holly didn't want to stall any longer. She found it creepy being in a deserted gallery in the middle of the night with a man wearing sunglasses. If she paid him, and he got away, she would personally take the amount out of Bono's hide.

She reached into the pocket of her jacket and pulled out the envelope full of cash. She handed it to him, expecting him to take out the money and count it, but he just looked inside the envelope and then transferred it to his own jacket pocket.

"Would you mind carrying it out to my car for me?" she asked him. Surely if the cops saw her leaving the building with a man carrying a canvas they would get the idea he was Sykol.

He lifted it down from the wall. "I guess you're probably disappointed. I really don't know what to say to people who buy my work."

"Your collages speak for you."

She saw the first hint of a smile on his face. "I'm glad you understand that. I hate selling to people who don't understand."

Holly opened the front door for him and followed him out. "It's the blue Chevy with the orange fenders," she told him.

Where the hell were the cops when she needed them?

She unlocked the car and pulled the seat forward so he could slide the canvas in. Just when there was nothing left for her to do but get in the car and drive off, two uniformed cops jumped out of the car parked in front of her and yelled, "Hold it right there, Sykol!"

Holly was just breathing a sigh of relief when Sykol panicked and made a run for it. The two cops took off after him and didn't catch him until he was rounding the corner. When they brought him back, in handcuffs, Holly was waiting for them.

"You sure took your time," she told them.

"Hey, we got him, didn't we?"

Sykol turned sunglassed eyes toward her. "You were in on this?"

"Nothing personal, but you stuck me with your bail."

"I what?"

"I'm your bail bondsperson."

"You?"

"Why not me?" asked Holly.

Sykol groaned. "Why didn't you just say so? I would've paid you."

"In what, phony twenties?"

"They're beautiful. Have you taken a look at them? They're art! While twenty-dollar bills are devaluating, mine are going to go up in value. They're an investment!"

"Sorry, Sykol, but I can't afford investments in art at the moment. I need to pay my rent." She turned to one of the cops. "He's got some money that belongs to me in an envelope in his pocket. The bills are marked, just in case you doubt me."

"That's not fair," said Sykol. "She's got my collage. I even discounted it for her."

Holly opened the car door and pushed the seat forward. She dragged out the canvas, being careful not to damage it. "Take it," she told Sykol. "I don't even like it."

Sykol was still muttering "Philistine" when she drove off.

HOLLY WAS TOO KEYED UP to sleep. If she were a guy she would've stopped by her neighborhood bar and had a drink. But women didn't show up alone in bars at three in the morning unless they were looking for more than a drink.

She decided to drive by her mother's house. Marilyn was a night owl, often staying up until dawn watching old movies on TV. She could make herself a cup of tea, tell her mother about Sykol, then head on home and sleep late in the morning. The week after New Year's there was usually a lull in crime anyway.

As she pulled into her mother's street, she saw a familiar car outside of her mom's house. What in hell was Bobby doing parked out there at three in the morning? If he was in there with her mother, she wasn't going in.

Holly pulled in behind Bobby's car and parked. She was just about to douse her headlights when she saw two heads appear above the seat and look back at the lights. Tiffany and Bobby? Parked? What in hell was going on?

Holly turned off the headlights and got out of the car. In the next second she was knocking at Bobby's window.

He rolled it down and in the light of the street lamps she could see his guilty look. "Hi, Holly," he said. Next to him, Tiffany was smoothing down her hair.

"What's going on here?" asked Holly.

"Nothing," said Bobby. "Tiffany was at the club tonight and I gave her a ride home, that's all."

Holly leaned down for a better look at Tiffany and saw that her sister's coat was in the back seat and her sweater was halfway to her neck. "Pull your sweater down, Tiffany," she said to her sister.

"Hey, we were just fooling around a little, you know how it is," said Bobby.

"No," said Holly. "Tell me how it is."

"We thought you'd be mad, Holly," said Tiffany.

"At what?" asked Holly.

The two of them exchanged glances. "We've been seeing each other," said Tiffany.

Holly crossed her arms. "Let me get this straight. I can't see Tom, but you two can see each other. Is that it?"

"Tiffany's not a witness," said Bobby.

"What do you think, I'm going to testify against my sister's boyfriend?" asked Holly. "Give me credit for a little family feeling, Bobby. Or is that why you're seeing her?"

"It wasn't like that at all," said Bobby. "It just happened."

"Well, it just happened between me and Tom, too. And now I can't see him, which is making me perfectly miserable, and you and Tiffany are out here enjoying yourselves.''

"It really doesn't seem fair, Bobby," said Tiffany.

"You really not going to testify against me?" asked Bobby.

"I might have to get on the stand, but I don't think anything I say will hurt you."

"See him," said Bobby. "I don't care. He's a good guy. I like him."

"What are you doing out at this hour?" asked Tiffany.

Holly told them about Sykol, but the one she really wanted to tell was Tom. And if she was hearing Bobby correctly, there was no reason why she couldn't. Right this minute if she felt like it.

"Well, I'll let you guys get back to it," she said, heading to her car.

Their heads had already disappeared from view by the time she passed them in the car. Bobby and Tiffany? It made sense in a perverse kind of way. Bobby always had liked hefty woman and Tiffany would be properly submissive; and she was getting the man she'd always wanted.

It was close to four when she pulled up in front of Tom's house. The entire street was dark, not even a night-light could be seen in any of the houses. She wondered if Tom liked pleasant surprises in the middle of the night. Well, she was soon going to find out.

She picked her way through the snow around to the back of the house where his bedroom window was located. She seemed to remember he slept with the window partly open.

It was open about three inches and she tried to push it open further. She had in mind climbing in and surprising him, but she couldn't get the window to push up any further. It was either stuck from the cold or he had some kind of locking device on it.

She was hitting the frame, trying to shake it loose, when a light went on and she could see Tom sitting up in bed.

"It's me," she said, so he wouldn't jump to the conclusion a burglar was trying to break into his house.

"Holly?" He got out of bed and came over to the window. "What're you doing out there?"

"I came by to see you."

"Why didn't you ring the doorbell?"

"At four in the morning?"

He tried to lift the window further but it wouldn't budge. "Would you have any objections to coming in the kitchen door?"

"None," said Holly, who was freezing to death by this time.

A moment later he had the kitchen door open and had pulled her inside and into his arms. "You're freezing," he said, letting go of her in a hurry.

"Can I spend the night?"

"I thought we agreed—"

"I got a dispensation from Bobby. I just drove by my mother's house and he and Tiffany were making out in his car."

Tom's face lit up. "Yeah?"

"Yeah. So he says it's okay for us to see each other."

"Just one thing," said Tom. "What're you doing out at this time of night?"

"That's a long story."

"I'm listening."

"Couldn't you listen just as well in bed?"

Tom grinned. "I don't see why not."

Interlude

On Saturday he came home from an antique auction he had attended on Long Island and found a manila envelope on his front porch. He squatted down to pick it up, being careful not to drop the Coca Cola sign he had purchased at the auction.

So she had been by while he was out and had dropped off her latest chapter. He wondered what would have happened if he had been home. Would she have spoken to him? Would she have come inside? Had she planned on returning to their home and resuming their married life and had his absence changed her mind?

He opened the door and went inside. He set the sign down on the hall table to take to work on Monday, then took the envelope into the living room and dropped it on the coffee table. He hung up his cotton jacket, got himself a beer and a bag of cheese puffs, and settled down on the couch for a read.

The first part, the part about Sykol, didn't interest him much. For one thing, he had heard all about it from her the night she tried to get in his bedroom window. For another, of course, he didn't appear in it, and he didn't think the story really moved except when they both were in it. On the other hand, he'd be going into the trial next, and that mostly concerned him. But trials were something people liked to read about. Everyone enjoyed a good trial. Going after a person who jumped bail just wasn't all that interesting. Anyway, they called these books romances, didn't they?

Still, who was he to say to leave it out? Let an editor tell her that it didn't move and she'd have to remove it. She'd listen to an editor.

He almost skipped the section on the Weight Watchers meeting just out of general principle. Good grief, people didn't want to read about that stuff, did they? There was no more boring subject in the world than diets. He'd grown up hearing about his mother's diets, and he didn't want to read about them, too.

He read it anyway, though, and a little bit into it he began to sense a trap. No way did she bring up that subject to her group way back then. It was this week she'd brought it up, he'd bet anything on it. And then she'd stuck it in just to get in some digs at him.

That character, that Deborah, complaining about her husband? There was no Deborah. That was *her*, complaining about *him*! Damn it, was that devious or what? Sending him messages through the manuscript? Why the entire book was going from thinly veiled fiction to out-and-out propaganda.

Give-and-take in marriage? He'd give her some give-and-take in marriage. He'd give her his two cents worth and she damn well better take it. As soon as he finished reading.

Well, she couldn't use the advice she gave to that Deborah because she didn't do all the cooking. They both cooked.

Oh, and now she was finally getting into her life with Bobby. Well, he bet there was a message in there, too, or else why throw it in when the book was almost finished?

What a bum the guy was. Who would have thought a nice guy like Bobby could've treated her so badly. The only thing he couldn't figure out was why she put up with it for eight years. He would've said "Bye, bye, I'm out of here" long before then.

But what did she know? The first guy she had ever gone out with? Maybe she figured any man would've treated her like that. He could remember a really fat girl in high school, the way if he happened to smile at her in the hall, she would blush with pleasure. He used to get a kick out of seeing her blush, never thinking about the pain he might have been causing her.

You just didn't think about fat kids having feelings in high school. You just figure that it was their fault they were fat, so why feel sorry for them. Even the guys were given a hard time, mostly because they were so inept at sports. The girls were ignored.

She must have been very unhappy before she met Bobby, and then she slowly found out that she still wasn't going to be happy. And it wasn't her fault she had been fat. She had been brought up to be fat. What a lot of courage it must have taken for her to take that first step. To join something like Weight Watchers and then stick to it until now she was so slim and pretty he couldn't even imagine her overweight. Sure, he'd seen pictures, but he hadn't really been able to relate the woman he knew to that fat girl in the flowing wedding dress.

In his own way, he'd given her just as hard a time as Bobby. He didn't ridicule her running, but never once

had he asked to join her. What did he think, it was
going to kill him to run a mile or two? He'd run in
high school and it hadn't killed him. Everyone was
running these days, he saw them everywhere. So
maybe he was healthy now, but somewhere down the
line he'd probably have to start worrying about his
heart rate and all of that. He knew for sure his father
was worrying these days. His dad had installed a
treadmill in the basement and used it twice a day reli-
giously. And one of his brothers played handball two
or three times a week.

Maybe he'd buy a treadmill. That way she wouldn't
even have to leave the house to run. They could set it
up with a TV set in front of it and take turns on it
during the news. It might even be kind of fun. The
way things were going, he was turning into a couch
potato.

Wait a minute. Just hold on a minute. She was saying, right there in black and white, that he ate like a
child. Now that was totally unfair. That was a low
blow. Just because he liked candy bars and ice cream
and potato chips, just because he preferred fast-food
places to sushi, just because— Well, come to think of
it, maybe he did eat like a child. But if that was the
case, why was it children got all the good things to eat?
If that stuff was so bad for him, why feed it to kids?

He guessed even the beer had something to do with
his childhood. He had started off drinking beer, and
then, when other guys were switching to vodka, and
then later to wine, and then later yet to Perrier with a
twist of lime, he was still drinking beer. The thing was,
he liked it. He liked the taste, he liked the relaxed way
it made him feel, and he also had the notion in the

back of his mind that beer was a lot healthier for you than hard liquor and that wine was for wimps.

Maybe he was drinking more than he should, though. A couple a night shouldn't hurt him any, but a lot of times he finished a six-pack. On weekends he usually went through a couple a day. Not that he couldn't hold it, but did he really need it? Wasn't it just about the same as pouring good money down the toilet?

He thought he must have picked up the habit when he'd been playing the comedy clubs. About all there was to do there was drink and watch the other comics, and then, to do his own act, he always needed a couple just to loosen up. Well, he wasn't a comedian now. There was absolutely no reason why a lawyer had to drink that much. He surely wouldn't show up for court after downing a few, not if he didn't want to be cited for contempt.

So okay. Maybe he could start eating and drinking more like an adult. Like an eighties adult, which was what he was. He could give her food a try—in larger portions, of course—and he could even switch to bottled water with his meals. Oh, hell, he could just use regular water. Hadn't New York City water tested out as pure and as tasty as the best bottled water on the market?

But first he'd finish up the beer he had in his hand while he read the rest of the chapter.

That night. That night had been so great he wished he could've written it from his point of view. There he was, falling more in love with her every day, only he couldn't see her and didn't even feel right about calling her. And then she'd shown up in the middle of the night at his bedroom window.

At first he'd thought it was someone trying to break into his house. His initial reaction had been that the guy had a lot of nerve breaking into a lawyer's house. His next thought had been that maybe, if he called the police and the guy was arrested, maybe he could defend him.

Then he had stopped thinking it was a burglar at all because if it was, it was the most inept burglar he'd ever heard about because the guy couldn't even get the window open.

When he'd heard her voice, it had been like he was still asleep. In his wildest dreams he hadn't had her showing up at his house in the middle of the night and trying to break into his bedroom.

It had been one of the greatest nights of his life, second only to Christmas Eve. He didn't think they got any sleep at all that night, they had been so busy talking and making love. He'd vowed then that he'd never let her go, and yet here they were, estranged, and he wasn't doing anything to get her back.

Well, all that was going to change starting right now!

He went out to the kitchen and got out one of the larger trash bags he used when he cleaned up the yard. He opened the kitchen cupboard and began to fill it with cookies and potato chips and crackers and all kinds of other things that a reasonable adult could live without. When the bag was full, he shook out a second one and began to empty the contents of the refrigerator and freezer. It wasn't easy getting rid of good food he had paid good money for, but if that's what it took to live in harmony with her, then it was a small price to pay.

He had a little trouble throwing out the beer. He finally compromised by leaving in one more can for today and two for Sunday. After that he'd try to go cold turkey.

He thought of putting the bags in his trunk and driving them to the dump. It wasn't that he didn't trust himself not to go out to the curb and undo them and retrieve some of the stuff he had thrown out, but why have temptation around?

No. That wasn't really necessary. It was a nice neighborhood, not the kind where people rooted around in their own trash. He'd feel really stupid if someone saw him doing that.

He'd just carry them out to the curb and forget all about them, and then he'd call her up and tell her he wanted her back. That he wanted her back so damn bad he could taste it. And if she said no, if she said she wasn't interested in coming back, then he could go back out to the curb and bring everything back in the house.

He was setting the bags on the curb when he saw her pull up in her multicolored Mustang, the one that wouldn't go more than thirty-five mph even if you floored it.

He stood back from the trash and watched her get out of the car.

She took a look at the bags and then took a look at him. "That's a lot of trash," she said.

"Yeah. I seem to accumulate it."

"I stopped by before with my chapter."

"I just finished reading it."

"I think maybe . . . well, I think maybe I should do some rewriting on it."

"It's fine the way it is."

She shook her head, avoiding his eyes. "No, it's not. I cheated."

"That's okay. I'll probably cheat on the courtroom scene and make myself look better than I was."

"It's just that the part at the meeting—"

"I know. I got your message. Look, no one's going to know the difference but us."

"You didn't mind?"

"A little bit maybe, at first. You want to come in?"

She looked around. "Half the neighbors are looking out their windows, wondering if we're getting back together."

"I'm wondering the same thing."

She didn't say anything to that, but she started for the house. When they got inside, she said, "There's something I want to say to you."

"Then let's talk," he said, heading for the living room. He thought it was a good sign when she sat down on the couch with him instead of taking one of the chairs.

Her eyes swept over the coffee table, and seeing only her chapter, became puzzled. She was no doubt wondering where the beer and the junk food were. He began to feel very proud of himself. Of course he could also use a beer, but what the hell?

"I've been doing a lot of thinking," she said, "and I've come to the conclusion that I can live with you just the way you are a lot better than I can live without you."

"I'll start driving you nuts again."

She shook her head. "You make me nervous sometimes, or rather some of the things you eat make me nervous. But I don't really think I'd give in and start eating that way again. Not seriously. I like myself too much the way I am. Anyway, everyone gets nervous about some things. A lot of people have jobs that make them nervous.''

"I used to get really nervous on the stage."

"And yet you loved it, right?"

"Yeah, I did," he said. "But I'll tell you something, I love you a lot more."

"I'm sorry I left like that."

"I'm sorry I let you. I should've straightened up right then."

"This isn't about straightening up. This is about learning to live with each other the way we are."

He thought about going out to the curb and bringing all his goodies back in. But then she said, "I don't see any food around," and he felt really proud of himself.

"What you said, about my eating like a child. I think you're right."

"Eating like a child isn't the worst thing in the world."

"I've decided to give adult behavior a try. I'm not making any promises, because maybe it won't work, but I'm going to give it my best shot."

She moved closer to him and he put his arm around her. "What was in those trash bags?"

"My childhood," he said, and then started laughing.

"All your food?"

"All except my weekend ration of beer and my Frosted Flakes."

She reached up and moved her hand through his hair the way he loved. "You are so good to me."

"Hell, I'm probably just being good to myself. In one fell swoop, I get both you and a healthier body. At least I better get a healthier body out of all this."

"You know something?" she asked.

"I love you, too."

"That goes without saying. What I was thinking, though, was do you realize we have only one chapter to go and our book is finished?"

"Already?"

"I would say so. I think the trial is the perfect way to end it."

"We really did it."

"I know. I never really thought we would."

"I'd say we've been very professional."

"At this rate, we could write a book every ten weeks."

"The only problem with that is," he said, "what do we write about?"

"I guess we'd have to think up stories."

"Which would take a whole lot longer."

"Oh, well, we've got all the time in the world."

He said, "You want to go out in the kitchen and check out the cupboards?"

"Not especially."

"Do you want to look in the empty refrigerator?"

She laughed. "We're going to have to do some grocery shopping."

"You want to go out to dinner? We can go to one of those fish places you like."

"Not right this minute."

"Well, let's see. You want to go into the bedroom and make mad, passionate love?"

"It's about time you got around to asking the right question."

Chapter Ten

Working on the assumption that male jury members would champion a guy who made a last-ditch stand at his ex-wife's Weight Watchers meeting, the prosecutor made every effort to load the jury with women. Tom deviously helped her in this effort. He was working on the assumption that women were likely to go for Bobby. And that if they didn't go for Bobby personally, they'd sympathize with such a grand gesture aimed at getting his true love back.

As it was, it was hard finding enough jurors who hadn't been influenced one way or the other by the vast amounts of publicity the case had received. Bobby was still making himself available to the press and drawing in large crowds at the Skylark Lounge. Conversely, Holly had antagonized the press by her persistent refusal to even make a statement. And Holly had somehow managed to put the lid on her mother's bent for publicity.

The day the trial began, Tom felt as nervous as the first time he'd done his comedy routine in front of an audience. He bought a new suit for the occasion, a charcoal-gray wool blend, narrowly cut, more Wall Street than Queens County Court. With it he wore a

white shirt and a rep tie and his best black shoes with
a good shine to them. He had been hoping the assistant D.A. would run true to form and dress in the
sloppy manner that was a hallmark of that office, but
Judith Green disappointed him. She was as well
dressed in a tailored wool suit and heels as she had
been well prepared in law school.

She and her three assistants entered the courtroom,
each carrying a bulging briefcase, making Tom feel all
alone at the defense table. He opened his not-so-
bulging briefcase, set some papers out on the table to
give it a professional look, then glanced over at Judith.

She grinned at him. "Ready to be demolished?" she
asked him, then carried a newspaper over and dropped
it on the table in front of him. "Terrorist Goes to
Trial" read the headline.

Tom pulled out his own morning paper and placed
it on top of hers. "Presley Impersonator's Plea: I did
it for love!" it said, and the rest of the page was taken
up with a picture of Bobby in satin and sideburns.

"Winner buys dinner?" asked Judith.

"You're on," said Tom, shaking on the bet.

Bobby was brought in, and on Tom's instructions
was wearing slacks, a camel wool sweater and a tweed
sport jacket. Tom's first choice for Bobby had been a
dark suit, but when he had seen Bobby in one, he
changed his mind. Bobby in a dark suit looked too
much like a hit man for the mob. In the sport jacket he
could conceivably be believed as an English professor
type if you didn't hear him speak.

The courtroom was packed with spectators. Marilyn and Tiffany Benson had arrived early and gotten
front row seats. Bobby's parents and assorted rela-

tives occupied a center section. There was a contingent of Bobby's loyal fans—all female—scattered around the room. Tom had tried to talk his family into coming, but none had professed an interest.

They all stood as the judge entered. Tom wasn't sure whether a female judge was good or bad. He had heard Patricia Wright was a tough judge; he was hoping she had a sense of humor. She might need a sense of humor with Bobby as the defendant.

When the jury filed in—eleven women and one lone man—their eyes immediately went to Bobby. "Smile at the jury," Tom whispered, nudging him.

Bobby dutifully smiled and eleven jurors smiled back. The man seemed to be reserving judgment. Judith caught this little bit of byplay and shot Tom a disgusted look. So it was a ploy? So what? Bobby was going to need all the help he could get.

Judith gave her opening address to the jury. She spoke of terrorism in the world at large and terrorism one night in Queens in particular. She made it sound as though Bobby were part of a worldwide conspiracy. Bobby looked over at her during one point, as though asking "Who, me?" and Tom saw sympathetic smiles on some of the jurors' faces.

She told the jury there was no question of Bobby's guilt. He was caught in the act in front of numerous witnesses. She said, with assurance, that she was certain the jury would agree with her and return a verdict of guilty. It sounded a bit like a closing address, but Tom didn't make any objections.

When it was Tom's turn, he spoke a lot about mitigating circumstances. They weren't going with the insanity plea in any form. Bobby had decided to say no to insanity. They were going with a trio of lesser defenses, such as uncontrollable impulse and lack of intent and muddled premeditation, none of which had a chance of holding up against a strong case from the prosecution. What they were actually doing was throwing Bobby on the mercy of the court. The trouble was, the judge didn't look all that merciful.

Judith called her first witness, the cop who had gotten the call from the Weight Watchers office the night of the alleged hostage situation. Tom looked over at Bobby and saw he was making eye contact with one of the plumper female jurors.

When it came time for him to question the witness, Tom asked him, "Did the telephone caller describe what was happening as a terrorist attack?"

"No," said the cop.

"What did she describe it as?"

"She just said there was a guy waving around a gun."

"Thank you," said Tom, throwing a satisfied look at the jury as though he had scored a point. Unfortunately, none of the jurors were even looking at him.

The prosecution appeared to have no dearth of witnesses. They brought out the ranking officer at the scene, a sniper, a SWAT team member, a hostage negotiator, everything but the mayor of New York. When they had all finished testifying, Tom had only one question: "When Mr. McKiever gave himself up, did he go with you peacefully?"

"Yeah, when he finally did it."

"Just a yes or a no will do."

"Yes."

Tom nodded again in satisfaction toward the jury. They were beginning to look bored.

"Good try," said Judith as she passed him on her way to call the next witness.

This was Maxine Gormley, the woman who had called the police. Since she was an associate of Holly's, Tom didn't think she'd do any real damage.

"Tell us, in your own words, what happened that night," said Judith.

"The meeting was in progress and I was just filing some membership forms when this man came into the office. He didn't look familiar, so I asked him what he wanted. I'm always afraid someone's going to come in and rob us some night."

"Did he look like a criminal to you?" asked Judith.

"He had a funny look in his eyes. But then he said he was Holly's husband—"

"He said 'husband'?"

"He might have said ex-husband," said Maxine, "I don't recall exactly. So I said she was in the meeting and he said he'd just go in there and wait for her. Then I went back to filing."

Maxine stopped speaking and looked out over the spectators, smiling at people she knew. Judith had to prod her. "Can you tell us what happened next?"

"Well, I got through filing, and I was going to leave early, do some last minute Christmas shopping. I stuck my head around the door to tell Holly I was leaving, and I see this man waving a gun. So naturally I screamed. And then I ran out of there and called the police. I didn't even stop to put on my coat."

Judith took her back over her story so many times that Tom felt his eyes beginning to droop. The courtroom was overheated and he hadn't slept well last night.

When it was his turn to cross-examine the witness, he said, "No questions." Judith had already elicited from the witness that she had been frightened of both the man and the gun and Tom didn't think he'd be able to get her to change her story in any substantial way. Anyway, he could tell the jury had had their fill of her and were ready to move on to something else.

Then came the long parade of Weight Watchers members who were there that night, which Tom was sure was going to culminate in Holly. She might be a hostile witness at this point, but she was still going to have to testify.

The witnesses had about the same ratio of men to women as the jury. Only one male witness took the stand, a chubby man named Arnold Bowers. He couldn't seem to say anything straight out, getting laughs from the jury with most of his testimony. Tom decided to take advantage of this good-natured attitude on cross.

"Tell me, Mr. Bowers," said Tom, "in one word, what was your impression of that night?"

"One word?" said Bowers. "Ridiculous."

Tom let that sink in with the jury. "Not frightening?"

"No, I'd have to go with ridiculous."

"Were you frightened when Mr. McKiever first came into your meeting?"

"Not at all."

"What about when he brought out the gun?"

Bowers shrugged. "At that point I figured it was a fake. The way things were going, I wouldn't have been surprised if it had shot water. Of course after he shot a hole through the ceiling I began to take it seriously."

"Take the situation seriously?"

"No, just the gun."

"Did it frighten you that you were being held hostage?"

"I figured I could walk out of there if I wanted to. I never believed he'd actually shoot anyone."

"Then why didn't you leave?"

"Listen, that was maybe the most interesting meeting I ever attended."

"Thank you, Mr. Bowers," said Tom, sharing his amusement with the jury.

At that point the judge announced a noon recess.

"THIS IS MAYBE the most open-and-shut case I ever had to prosecute, and it's turning into a circus," said Judith, methodically picking all the mushrooms out of her salad.

"So what do you think, Judith? You think all those female jurors are horrified by a Weight Watchers meeting being held hostage?"

"I should have known something was up during jury selection."

"I just figured the females would go for Bobby."

"Some of them are professional women. How could they be so easily taken in?"

"You were getting into his Elvis act."

"But he's not Elvis now. Actually, I was expecting you to have him dress up in satin."

"Give me credit for a little class, Judith."

Judith didn't look convinced.

SITUATION COMEDY was the order of the afternoon. Sylvia, one of the witnesses, interspersed her testimony with one-liners that had even the judge smiling.

She didn't bother looking at the attorneys when they were questioning her; she played straight to the jury and had them in her hands.

Tom only had one question for her.

"So you found the whole thing highly romantic?"

"Definitely," said Sylvia. "My husband should be so romantic as to hold me hostage."

The spectators cracked up.

The rest of the alleged hostages were equally blasé about the hostage situation. Most agreed it had been one of their most memorable experiences. None held a grudge against Bobby. As the testimony continued, Bobby's rooting section among the spectators had to be cautioned twice by the judge, who threatened to clear the courtroom if they didn't quit shouting their approval.

The last witness to take the stand for the prosecution was Holly. She should have been expected to be the prosecution's star witness. Tom figured Judith still felt she could elicit what she wanted from Holly despite the fact that she was now a hostile witness.

Holly went along with her up to a point. To the question, "Did you think this was normal behavior on the part of your ex-husband?" she answered, "I never expect the normal from Bobby."

Tom heard a growl coming from Bobby. Afraid his client was going to make a scene in court, Tom wrote "Shut Up" on his legal pad and shoved it over where Bobby could read it.

Judith pressed the point. "So Mr. McKiever is prone to criminal behavior?"

"Not criminal," said Holly, "just bizarre."

Laughter erupted in the courtroom.

"Tell me," said Judith, "were you frightened at any point?"

"I was angry. I was frustrated. No, I wasn't frightened. Bobby has a big mouth, but there's nothing behind it."

"Why don't you object to that?" Bobby asked him.

"Why don't you shut up?" whispered Tom.

Tom really had no pertinent questions for Holly, but he wanted to talk to her so much he didn't want to miss any opportunity. It had been two days since he'd seen her and a day since they'd spoken.

He approached the witness chair and smiled at her. She smiled back. She was looking pretty professional herself in a gray suit and a pink blouse and gray suede boots that went up to her knees.

"Ms. Benson," he began, and saw a gleam come into her eyes. "Would you tell this court whether at any time during the alleged hostage situation you felt in any danger from your ex-husband?"

"He was more in danger from me," said Holly. "At a couple of points I felt like killing him."

"Objection," shouted Judith.

"Sustained," said the judge. "Just answer the question, please."

"No," said Holly.

"At any time before or after the hostage situation, have you ever felt in physical danger from Mr. McKiever?"

"No," said Holly.

"Do you feel he's a danger to the public at large?"

"Only to himself," muttered Holly, and then, when Judith started to object, she quickly amended her answer to no.

Tom smiled at her again. "Thank you, Ms. Benson."

Judith jumped up with one more question. "Ms. Benson, do you think your ex-husband should be punished for his behavior?"

"Not relevant," objected Tom.

"I'd like to hear the answer to that," said the judge.

Holly looked cornered for a moment. She was under oath and Tom could see she was struggling with her conscience over answering that truthfully. She finally said, "Yes."

Bobby let out a groan and the spectators seated right behind him chuckled. Tom saw that the jury wasn't agreeing with her, though; some of them were now viewing Holly with outright hostility.

"The prosecution rests," said Judith, sweeping past Tom without a glance.

"Is the defense ready?" asked the judge.

"Yes, your honor," said Tom. He might have asked for an early adjournment, but since the only witness he was calling was Bobby, he decided not to stretch it into a second day if it wasn't necessary. "I call the defendant, Robert McKiever, to the stand."

"Quit playing to the jury," Tom admonished his client before he took the stand. "It's not going over well with the judge."

"I'll be cool," said Bobby.

"Make sure you are. I think we have it won, so don't screw it up."

He had second thoughts about letting Bobby testify for himself. Judith could easily elicit damaging information from him that Tom didn't know about. Or Bobby could get so cocksure that the jury could become disenchanted. But if he didn't call him, he was certain that the jury would feel cheated. Bobby appeared to be the star of the show and the jury wanted to hear the star.

Bobby swaggered up to the witness chair and was sworn in. When he had taken his seat, Tom approached him. "Mr. McKiever, I'm going to ask you to tell the court, in your own words, just what happened the night of the alleged hostage situation."

Bobby, well rehearsed, turned a sheepish grin first on the judge, then on the spectators, and lastly on the jury. "Well, let me say first of all that I behaved really stupidly. All I can say in miti . . . miti . . ."

"Mitigation," Tom prompted him.

"Yeah, in mitigation, is that I'm really sorry for all the trouble I've caused everyone and if I had it to do over, I sure wouldn't do it."

Tom could see the jury was with him.

"I had it in mind, see, to get my ex-wife to come back to me. I had tried to see her, but she wouldn't see me. I kept calling her, but she wouldn't pick up the phone or answer my messages. Finally, believing that if I could just get her alone and talk to her, I could get her to come back to me—" And he was off and running as the jury watched breathlessly and the reporters scribbled in their notebooks.

THE JURY WAS OUT exactly twenty minutes, which was just about the amount of time the bailiff would've needed to get them all a cup of coffee. Tom hadn't even left the building yet when he was called back in.

Judith paused at his table long enough to say, "This is the most ridiculous case I've ever tried."

"I'm looking forward to dinner," Tom said with a grin.

Bobby was brought in, also complaining about the length of his break. "It's gotta be good news," Tom told him. "If they were going to convict, they would have been out a lot longer. Hell, it would've taken days for the others to convince that one who's already in love with you."

When the verdict of not guilty was read, the courtroom went crazy. Over the yelling and the cheering, the judge thanked the jury and dismissed them, then left the courtroom herself.

One jury member took the dismissal seriously. The other members—those of the female variety—surrounded Bobby, all of them requesting his autograph.

Judith came over and shook his hand, and then Bobby was turning around and clasping him in a hug, saying, "Hey, buddy, you did it! You're a great lawyer, you know that?"

"Then you won't mind the size of my bill," said Tom.

"Double it! I don't mind."

Tom saw Tiffany shoving her way through the crowd to get to Bobby. He quickly said to Bobby, "Listen, I have a confession to make."

"To *me*?" asked Bobby.

"I'm in love with your ex-wife."

"That's great," said Bobby. "I understand from Tiffany that it's mutual."

Tom was feeling euphoric when he got outside the courtroom and was surrounded by the press. He had won his first criminal case; he was on his way.

He answered all their questions, posed in front of the TV cameras with Bobby, then spotted Holly across the street trying to blend in with a lamppost.

He crossed over to her. "You avoiding the press?" he asked her.

"Bunch of vultures," said Holly.

"But lovely vultures today," said Tom. "Let's go home. I want to see myself on the news."

"You mean 'home' as in *your* house?"

He put his arm around her. "Why not? Is there anything stopping us from getting married now that the trial is over?"

"Not a thing in the world," said Holly, "except I don't recall your asking me."

"I got Bobby's permission."

"What!"

"Only kidding. But I told him I was in love with you and he thought it was great."

"Speak of the devil," said Holly, and Tom turned to see Bobby crossing the street with Tiffany in tow. Tom figured Bobby must have been pretty slick to get rid of his fans that fast.

"Hey, you guys," said Bobby. "I just had this great thought. How about we have a double wedding?"

"You're getting married?" Holly asked Tiffany.

Tiffany glowed with happiness. "He just asked me."

Holly crossed her arms. "Tom hasn't exactly asked me yet."

Bobby, who had no time for small details like that, said, "Think of all the publicity we'd get with a double wedding."

"I think it's a perfectly awful idea," said Holly. "It would be like incest."

"Not really incest," said Tom.

"Can you see the newspapers?" asked Holly. "Ex-husband marries ex-sister-in-law while ex-husband's defense attorney marries ex-husband's ex-wife? It would be in the worst possible taste.''

"Mother would adore it," said Tiffany.

"Well, I'm sorry," said Holly, "but that isn't the way I want to get married."

"How do you want to get married?" Tom asked her.

"Quietly. Preferably out of town."

"Does that mean you'll marry me?"

"Are you asking me to marry you?"

"I'm asking you, Holly."

"Then yes, I will."

Tiffany burst into tears. "Isn't that beautiful?" she asked Bobby. "He won his case and my sister, both on the same day."

Epilogue

"We've done it!" she said, putting down the pages and letting out the kind of cheer usually reserved for rock concerts. "We've really done it!"

"You liked the new ending?"

"Oh, yes, it's much better. You couldn't end the book with the verdict."

"I imagine some books end that way."

"Yes, but not romances. Romances end with the hero asking the heroine to marry him. That's the real story, after all, not the trial. If the trial was the main story, then Bobby would've been the hero."

"They all end the same way? Everyone ends up married?"

"Well, they used to. Times have changed and nowadays they sometimes end up moving in together, but you always know, sometime in the future, that they're going to get married."

"We moved in together."

"Yes, but the readers won't know that. And anyway, we did get married."

She set down the papers and moved over to the couch. She had had to move off the couch when she was reading because he kept reading over her shoulder and making her nervous.

He said, "It's funny, isn't it? Bobby and Tiffany eloped, and we're the ones who ended up having a big wedding."

"You hadn't told me what an extensive family you had. Or how much your mother was looking forward to a wedding."

"You hadn't even met my mother."

"Exactly."

He was silent for a moment. "She tries."

"Indeed she does." The subject of his mother not interesting her very much, she quickly changed it. "You know what I think? I think we deserve a bottle of champagne. Do you realize we've actually written a book? Together? And that it's finished?"

"We don't have any champagne. We don't even have any beer."

"Then we shall go out to eat. A celebratory dinner, someplace expensive and wonderful. Probably we should go to one of those well-known places in Manhattan where all the famous writers hang out, although I'd gladly settle for The Hamptons, and the beach crowds aren't there just yet."

"That'll mean dressing up."

"Oh, I don't think it's necessary in The Hamptons. Anyway, the rich and the famous don't *have* to dress up."

He chuckled. "Is that how you envision us?"

"Well, maybe not immediately."

"Do you have any idea how much a book like this would bring?"

"None at all," she said. "But I've always had the idea those romance writers were very rich. Maybe it's because they write so many books."

"I was thinking..."

"Yes?"

"Nothing. Well, shall we go to The Hamptons?"

"Not until you tell me what you were thinking."

He grinned. "I'm sorry I said it."

"I can see you are. Go on, tell me. I want to know what you were thinking."

"I was thinking that I'll miss this."

"You sound like you're going off to war or something."

"I'm talking about the writing. I'll miss it. I'll miss reading your chapters, getting your view of things, and I'll also miss the writing. I didn't think I would, but I actually enjoyed it."

"I did, too. And I'll miss reading yours, even if we did argue about it half the time."

"So what do you think? Should we do another?"

"Do you have a story in mind?"

He gave her a rather sly smile. "You might not like this."

"I won't if you keep smirking at me like that."

"I just thought—you probably won't agree—but couldn't we write a sequel?"

"You mean about us?"

"Why not?"

"Look, I find us endlessly fascinating, too, but I don't know whether there's a story there."

"It seemed like a story at the time."

"You mean about our problems?"

He nodded.

"You really want to expose yourself like that? Anyone you know might read it."

"You talk as though I were a closet alcoholic. I'm not ashamed of putting away a few beers and some junk food. I bet a lot of people could empathize with that."

"I just don't think it's that interesting. Anyway, these books aren't supposed to be about married couples."

"Is that a rule?"

"Married couples just aren't interesting."

"Are you telling me that we've suddenly gotten boring since we've been married?"

"No, of course not. But there's no story. No love story. If it starts off with us in love and if it ends with us in love, and all the way through we were in love, where's the conflict?"

He grinned. "Conflict? Have you been reading those books about writing again?"

"Well, we can't continue faking it. Somewhere down the road we're going to have to learn a few things."

"That case I'm going to trial with in a couple of weeks, that might make a good story."

"But not a love story. Unless something's going on with your client I don't know about."

"Do you have any better ideas?"

She wished she had, but she hadn't actually given any thought to writing another book. Where did people come up with all those ideas, anyway? Once you've used up your own life, where do you go from there? "I don't have any ideas at all," she admitted.

"Then I say we go for a sequel."

"I think it's a waste of time. I think this book is good, I really do, and I think there's a possibility of our selling it. But I think if we write a sequel no one's going to be interested in it."

"I think you're wrong," he said. "Maybe it's not your standard romance, but it's a hell of a good story. It's kind of a domestic comedy. You see them in the movies all the time."

"Jack Nicholson could certainly play your part."

"What do you mean by that?"

"I don't think I've ever seen the man in a movie where he wasn't drinking."

"I resent that. Anyway, he's too old. Meryl Streep would be perfect as you, though."

"I've suddenly gone from Sissy Spacek to Meryl Streep?"

"She's so slim. And I could see her holding forth at those meetings of yours. Anyway, Jack Nicholson is too strong for Sissy Spacek—he'd demolish her."

She was starting to get into it. "You know who'd be perfect for Bobby? Dustin Hoffman."

"He's too old."

"They're all too old."

"Anyway, Bobby wouldn't even be in it. Oh, maybe as a minor character, but Dustin Hoffman wouldn't take such a small part."

She started to laugh. "You know what? We're beginning to sound as though we're going to write a screenplay, not a book."

He didn't join in the laughter. "Why not?"

"Why not what?"

"Why *don't* we write a screenplay?"

"I don't know the first thing about writing a script."

"We didn't know anything about writing books, either."

"Yes, but I read books."

"You also see movies."

She gave him a long look. "Do you really think we could do it?"

"Why not? We'll get a book to see what the format is, and then go on from there."

"I'm sure it's too difficult."

He put his arm around her. "Listen to you. You thought nothing of writing a book. If we can do that, maybe we can do anything."

"But what would we do after the sequel?" she asked. "Our lives aren't exciting enough to write about."

"Then we'll have to start having some adventures."

"Or we'll have to start using our imaginations."

He put his other arm around her and pulled her close. "I have a pretty vivid imagination. You know what I'm imagining right now?"

"I could make a pretty good guess. But I thought we were going out to eat?"

"I could always go up to the corner and get a bottle of champagne."

"And we could celebrate in bed?"

He grinned.

"I guess we could go out for Sunday dinner instead."

"No reason why not."

"You know something? You know what those books never tell you?"

"What's that?" he asked.

She moved in closer to him. "That the honeymoon just goes on and on."

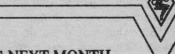

Harlequin American Romance

COMING NEXT MONTH

Harlequin Temptation dares to be different!

Once in a while, we Temptation editors spot a romance that's truly innovative. To make sure *you* don't miss any one of these outstanding selections, we'll mark them for you.

EDITOR'S CHOICE

When the "Editors' Choice" fold-back appears on a Temptation cover, you'll know we've found that extra-special page-turner!

THE

Temptation

EDITORS

Have You Ever Wondered If You Could Write A Harlequin Novel?

Here's great news—Harlequin is offering a series of cassette tapes to help you do just that. Written by Harlequin editors, these tapes give practical advice on how to make your characters—and your story— come alive. There's a tape for each contemporary romance series Harlequin publishes.

Mail order only

All sales final